THE BLUNDER

THE BLUNDER

A NOVEL

MUTT-LON

TRANSLATED BY AMY B. REID

AMAZON CROSSING

Text copyright © 2020 by Mutt-Lon
Translation copyright © 2022 by Amy B. Reid
All rights reserved.

Previously published as *Les 700 aveugles de Bafia* by Éditions Emmanuelle Collas in France in 2020. Translated from French by Amy B. Reid. First published in English by Amazon Crossing in 2022.

Published by Amazon Crossing, Seattle

www.apub.com

Amazon, the Amazon logo, and Amazon Crossing are trademarks of Amazon.com, Inc., or its affiliates.

ISBN-13: 9781542037877 (hardcover)
ISBN-10: 1542037875 (hardcover)

ISBN-13: 9781542037853 (paperback)
ISBN-10: 1542037859 (paperback)

Cover design by Laywan Kwan

Printed in the United States of America

First edition

To those who are overwhelmed and tempted to give up,
and to those who overwhelm them.

Contents

AUTHOR'S NOTE
FOR THE ENGLISH TRANSLATION

The Blunder is a work of fiction layered over an actual historical event. Dr. Eugène Jamot was a French physician who led a campaign to combat trypanosomiasis, sleeping sickness, in Cameroon between 1922 and 1931. The archives confirm that his medical organization was responsible for a wide-scale case of medical malpractice, a "blunder" that led to hundreds of cases of blindness in villages across the region of Bafia. In my novel, I draw on this unbelievable fact to set my plot in motion, with fictional characters, such as my two female protagonists, Damienne Bourdin and Edoa Débora, alongside individuals who played central roles in the historical moment.

During this time, after World War I, Cameroon was a territory under control of the League of Nations, the precursor to the United Nations, with Great Britain and France administering separate parts of the former German colony and serving as de facto colonizing powers. Our story plays out in the French region. The colonists lived alongside local populations, composed of both Bantus and Pygmies.

Throughout this tale, the voices and expressions we hear, and the actions described, reflect the characters' points of view, how they understood their roles in the African colonies in that time period, when racism and prejudice were codified. The word "native"—*indigène* in

French—was a legal classification for the local populations, and the white colonizers were firmly convinced of their own superiority and of France's "civilizing mission." However, there were also ethnic hierarchies at play among the local people, with the Bantus seeking to assert their superiority over the Pygmies. As a result, readers should feel a certain discomfort with different episodes in the novel, but that reflects my efforts to faithfully reproduce the context of this moment in Cameroon's past.

Mutt-Lon
September 2021

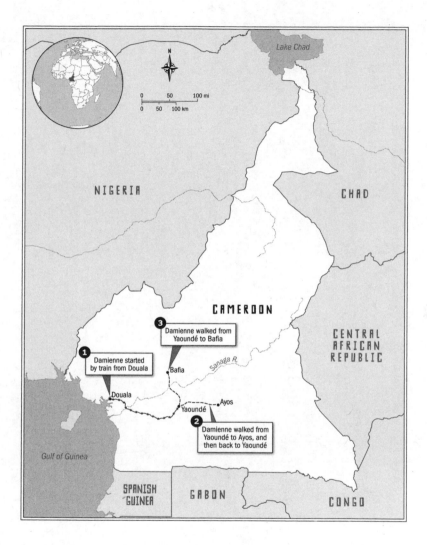

NIGERIA

CHAD

CAMEROON

CENTRAL AFRICAN REPUBLIC

① Damienne started by train from Douala

③ Damienne walked from Yaoundé to Bafia

Bafia

Sanaga R.

Douala

Ayos

Yaoundé

② Damienne walked from Yaoundé to Ayos, and then back to Yaoundé

Gulf of Guinea

SPANISH GUINEA

GABON

CONGO

Lake Chad

N

0   50   100 mi
0   50   100 km

The Return

Damienne Bourdin's first priority, as she emerged from the airport, was to track down the Pygmy guide who'd saved her life in 1929. She hadn't set foot in Cameroon for thirty-two years, and wondered if it might be a waste of time to look for him. Most of the protagonists of the "blunder" were no longer living, and the guide might have died, too, like Dr. Jamot and Chief Atangana. It was important she find out, because if that strange fellow was still alive, Damienne wouldn't dare return to the scene of the revolt without him.

The *France-Soir* she was leafing through mentioned a monument in honor of Dr. Jamot in front of the Ministry of Public Health and also the facilities he'd left behind in 1931, now a hospital bearing his name. In the taxi on the way to the hospital, she kept her nose glued to the window. How Yaoundé had changed! There was asphalt in the city center, electricity, a big traffic circle, and people weren't wandering around in loincloths. Some blocks of houses still had mud walls, but only a few were thatched or had roofs covered in straw or woven raffia mats. Buildings were going up, Peugeots and Renaults racing around them every which way, like ants. Drivers shouted through open windows as they passed each other on either side, but Damienne didn't mind the chaos, she was just relieved she wouldn't have to walk the whole way to Bafia this time.

The area around the hospital was completely transformed, not one landmark from her time there survived. Still, Damienne recognized the hospital itself right away. She noticed as she approached that no additions had been made; at most, they'd slapped a coat of lime on a few walls. Inside, she found that Dr. Jamot's apartment had become the radiology department, and the room where she'd spent the night was now a pulmonologist's office. Since sleeping sickness had been largely eradicated, the Jamot Hospital focused on psychiatry and fighting tuberculosis—there were sickly people with emaciated faces everywhere. Damienne offered a prayer that this new prevention campaign, unlike the last, would be blunder free, and that no other French doctor would experience what she'd lived through under Dr. Jamot.

The director of the hospital was reading a newspaper, its front page dedicated to President Kennedy, assassinated six days earlier. He greeted Damienne with the particular courtesy reserved for those who regularly appear in the press. He was honored to meet her, he'd read almost all of her books, and particularly loved the last one, about the Jamot Mission, for which she'd won numerous prizes. Since the book was about to be made into a film, he offered to put the hospital facilities at the disposal of the film crew. Damienne was obliged to answer all his admiring questions, and even accept an invitation for dinner with him and his wife, before she could raise the subject she had come to discuss. Was the Pygmy still alive? After what felt like an eternity, the director gathered all the hospital personnel together, and they found an old nurse who said he'd met Ndongo, the Pygmy in question. The nurse had last seen him toward the end of the 1930s, before Ndongo went home to Bipindi.

So Damienne went to Bipindi to look for him. Bipindi was in a part of the bush that hadn't changed for thousands of years, and Damienne thought to herself that, in some ways, the town seemed more backward than the remote villages she'd gone through back in 1929. Here, every-one was a hunter, even the women, and no one needed to go far from their home to hunt game. One inquiry and two false leads later, the Pygmy was found. Ndongo was alive. When at last she saw him, Damienne hugged and kissed him without hesitation, and burst into tears before his whole surprised clan. Ndongo hadn't changed much, still wiry and stunted, but now an old man. Like Damienne's, the skin on his hands was paper thin. He lived with his wife and children in *mungulus*, huts made of branches and green leaves, which she'd once seen him build in just a few minutes, on that unforgettable day when they were lost in the forest . . .

What struck her most was his attire: Ndongo still wore a loincloth fashioned from an animal hide. He was bare chested and had the same amulets tied around his waist and biceps as he'd worn on the day they'd said farewell. She couldn't believe it! In his small, lively eyes, Damienne saw a flash of that primitive man she remembered so well. There was one remarkable change: Ndongo spoke French. She was almost chagrined that she no longer needed to act things out for him.

He agreed to go with her to Bafia.

Despite the muddy swamps, rickety bridges, and a tired old ferry, the road from Yaoundé to Bafia seemed like a vision of futuristic infrastruc-ture compared to the one Damienne had traveled years before. Trucks now regularly carried goods along the route; it took just half a day to traverse the 120 kilometers between the two towns. Of course, some-times a truck would get stuck in the mud and the passengers would be invited to push it all through the night; but other than shepherds leading their flocks, no one traveled on foot.

As they arrived in Bafia, Damienne's heart started pounding. The scent of cas mango, the delicious fruits with spikey pits, was overwhelm-ing, just as before. There were a few old familiar huts—leaning, just as before, but still standing—with their cracked earthen walls, woven mats hanging over windows and doors, roofs that miraculously stayed on after each gust of wind. Overall, though, cement blocks and corrugated metal seemed to be winning out. Coming into town, they saw the seed of a small town center with shops, a pharmacy, a bus station, even a bank!

The Pygmy hadn't lost his guiding reflexes; he pointed toward the road leading up to the former residence of the colonial administrator, and together they started off. The streets were filled with a new generation of citizens wearing shirts, trousers, and shoes. They checked the time with a glance at their wrist and even went to school instead of spending their days hunting. They could live and flourish without fear of trypanosomiasis. Damienne wondered if anyone had ever told them about the dreadful sleeping sickness that had decimated their ancestors, and perhaps even some close relatives. Were they aware of the preventive war fought to save them? Had they learned of the terrible blunder and the native revolt that followed? Thirty years later, there were undoubtedly still some who had been blinded by the Jamot Affair left in the villages in and around Bafia. Damienne remembered some who at the time weren't yet twenty years old. Among the youth of today, some were surely their children and grandchildren, and maybe they'd told them what the Jamot Mission had done to them. A truth banned from history books.

The residence of the colonial administrator was there, unchanged, its gabled roof covered in red tiles, a raised veranda running along the front, and three windows with their wide wooden shutters. It had been repurposed as offices for the subprefecture. Two horses were grazing peacefully in the spacious courtyard. Damienne stood at the edge of the courtyard, precisely where she'd seen angry natives covered in paint and dancing on a steamy morning in December 1929 while she hid behind the shutter of the middle window, trapped inside with the others. She wanted to go into the main building, to stare hard at the cement floor of that living room where she thought she'd lose her life, check if the marks where spears flew against the walls were still visible, and glance into the kitchen where Sikini, the woman who'd let Damienne wear her pagne, had worked so hard. She wanted to walk through the residence once more, but paralyzed by her painful memories, she couldn't go any farther, and opted instead to head back toward the center of town and look for the health center.

Damienne had to circle around several times before finding the place where Dr. Monier had lived and worked. The site had been divided up, and now a restaurant served hedgehog and crocodile on the very spot where once stood the health center for the subdivision of Bafia. No mention of the fire, no trace of Madame Monier's garden. Nothing. It was disheartening to see people gnawing away at a hedgehog, seemingly unaware of the historic events that had played out there. Because this is where it started, the long list of victims that upended the whole region, the local colonial administration, and even the Ministry of the Colonies in Paris! Damienne longed to tear down the sign of the restaurant, Le Biabérebé, and replace it with a plaque bearing the following inscription: *Here was born the scandal that carried off Dr. Eugène Jamot.*

She had dreamed of this pilgrimage for decades. But now, though it had barely begun, Damienne was already weary. Professional success and a comfortable life had blunted the fury to please that had made her almost impossible to live with in her younger years. She had lost the quasi-mystical faith that had let her survive so many shipwrecks. Perhaps that's why, after receiving Sikini's letter, Damienne had finally agreed to come back to Cameroon, to retrace her steps and relive, if only in her mind, that fateful and chaotic time of her life, when she had nothing to wager and yet so much to lose.

And it was working. She was all atingle, and her memories came flooding back in a torrent.

I: The Blunder

On that morning in December 1929, François Bertignac was in a pleasant mood, and for good reason: it was his last medical inspection in the village of Donenkeng. Just two more weeks in the bush and he'd be on the boat back to France and his native Auvergne. During the years he'd been in Cameroon, he'd served tirelessly as a health auxiliary in the preventive mission led by Dr. Jamot, and he was proud of that. It was thanks to him, and people like him, that the locals were being delivered from sleeping sickness. Bertignac firmly believed that out of all the jobs in the African colonies, none was more challenging than that of health auxiliary. Each day, he trekked dozens of kilometers, on foot, to remote villages to check on ailing natives, who were illiterate and often skeptical of the White Man's medicine. For four long years, Bertignac lived and worked in the heart of this tsetse-infested jungle, and when he finally got sleeping sickness himself, he believed he'd never see his family again. He'd received the same treatment as the natives, and luckily, it had worked, with no adverse side effects. As his African colleagues set up their folding tables and laid out their equipment, Bertignac thought about the last letter he'd gotten from the one he no longer dared to think of as his fiancée. That was over two years ago, in May 1927. Now, in two short weeks, he'd try to win her back. He'd move mountains to do it.

Donenkeng was quiet, as usual. Since the first miraculous cures in the region, the white doctors enjoyed a certain level of esteem. They visited the villages on a strict schedule. The day before their arrival, the natives, usually so eager to be helpful, prepared by building the shelter where the medical team would set up shop. They had learned to line up, organized by sex and age, before the doctors even arrived.

So Bertignac was surprised when he saw no one lined up in the main courtyard. It was already ten in the morning. He wasn't too worried, though, since the shelter had been built. After years of living among these people, whose language he spoke fairly well, Bertignac knew that many things could explain finding a native village empty: some interfamilial dispute to be settled, or a ritual the day before that had gone on to the early morning hours, or, simply, a general disregard for time. On that last point, Bertignac had come to a strongly held belief: lack of punctuality was a trait shared by all tribes in Black Africa, just like palavers and procrastination.

Once the native nurses had finished setting up, Bertignac blew his whistle several times to draw people out of their huts. Finally the court-yard filled and lines formed in front of the medical shelter. Bertignac, as head of the unit, checked that everything was in order, and then the examinations began.

He was helping the nurse giving injections fill the first syringes when a woman ran across the courtyard and spoke to him in Bafia, the local dialect. She was exhausted and anxious. Bertignac recognized her, and the secretary-interpreter confirmed she was the youngest wife of the first notable of the village, who was also the chief's eldest son. No one needed to translate, Bertignac understood that she wanted him to go to her husband's bedside. That was convenient, since he lived in a hut within the chief's compound, and Bertignac had already planned on going there. He promised he would do as she asked as soon as he was finished with the village chief. In Donenkeng the chief came first, and no one would have dared to suggest otherwise.

The chief's younger son was waiting for Bertignac at the entrance to the compound; he seemed cold and distant. *Nothing strange in that*, Bertignac thought; he knew the fellow wasn't quick to smile.

Together they went into the chief's bedroom.

The chief had survived sleeping sickness, thanks to Dr. Monier's care. Bertignac had met him many times, but this was only the fifth time he'd examined him—he was filling in after Dr. Monier's departure. The chief, at least eighty-five at this point, had been blind for eight months. He was the very first case of blindness reported in the subdivision. Bertignac knew why he'd lost his sight, and he also knew he'd never get it back, but it wasn't his job to tell him. Besides, Dr. Monier, head of the subdivision's health service, never spoke of it with anyone. Even Dr. Jamot, in charge of the whole preventive mission, who had examined the old man just one month earlier during his big inspection tour, had said nothing to him. Truth be told, there was nothing that could be done for him, besides keeping his spirits up. Communicating through his son, Bertignac promised him for the fifth time that his sight would soon return and, to boost his confidence, had him drink some cough syrup. No one could have imagined that would be the last thing that the old man ever consumed; when Bertignac left the bedroom, he was talking normally with his son.

In the living room of the chief's compound, Bertignac saw the woman who'd approached him earlier, so, as promised, he went to her husband's bedside. The chief's younger son followed as Bertignac was led to a room where a naked man was laid out on a bed. A healer was leaning over the patient and massaging something on his groin with a smoking bundle of leaves. Bertignac was overcome with horror when he realized that it was an enormous boil, red and raw. Worse, the wound had been slathered with a dubious-looking ointment. Bertignac quickly cleaned the boil, as well as the patient's thigh. Covered in a nauseating layer of sweat, the man was too weak to even moan; his body racked with spasms, his limbs growing stiffer and stiffer. Despite his gaping mouth and apparent paralysis, Bertignac's diagnosis was immediate. This wasn't another case of sleeping sickness. He had tetanus. Bertignac pulled something from his medical kit and gave the patient an injection. After forbidding the younger brother from massaging his joints, he left the chief's compound.

When Bertignac rejoined the other members of his unit in the courtyard, the nurse Mongui, who was giving injections, was overwhelmed. He was a good-hearted young man, but lacked the talent of his colleagues, who had more experience. After checking for swollen lymph nodes and taking fluid samples and analyzing them under a microscope, they wrote their diagnoses in chalk on each patient's chest and sent them all to Mongui, who would administer the appropriate treatment. To prevent a backlog at Mongui's table, Bertignac gave him a hand for half an hour or so.

Just as he was heading to his own post to begin giving vaccinations, the unit leader heard screams and crying from the chief's compound. At first, no one seemed worried; just a woman crying; nothing more banal than that in this village where it was common to beat your wives, even in public. Bertignac vaccinated his first patient. He had just started lecturing the second when three hysterical women rushed from the chief's compound, arms raised to the sky. They sat on the ground and began bouncing on their bare behinds—their movements looked almost choreographed—while howling and slapping their thighs. Immediately, the courtyard exploded. Everyone waiting in line rushed to join the mourning women. The clamor was infernal. Even the dogs were barking.

Bertignac realized that tetanus had claimed another victim. For him, there was no doubt: it was the healer's fault, he'd infected the boil with those dubious ointments. As he silently cursed the healer, the chief's younger son appeared in the courtyard and headed toward him, but was stopped by a notable who whispered something in his ear and, taking his arm, pulled him back to the chief's compound. The younger son reluctantly followed the notable back through the crowd, staring angrily at Bertignac the whole time. The doctor turned to his native colleagues. They were distraught, their faces strained, practically in tears. Suddenly he felt strangely alone.

A short time later, the same notable returned and announced solemnly that the chief's elder son was dead, and that upon hearing the news, the old sovereign had also succumbed. Collective hysteria broke out.

The younger son emerged from the chief's compound and strode toward the shelter. Bertignac, familiar with native ways, knew he had reason to worry. The man planted himself in front of him and spat on the ground. Pointing an accusing finger at him, the younger son proclaimed the health auxiliary his brother's assassin. He described in detail how Bertignac had wiped away all the remedies prepared by a respected healer, and how the Frenchman had forbidden him from massaging his brother's limbs as he grew stiff. Since no native knew that it's unadvisable to handle a tetanus patient more than necessary, Bertignac had no defense. The younger son then insisted Bertignac was also complicit in the death of his father, the old chief, because his blindness had not been natural, but a plot orchestrated by the white colonists against the African people. He didn't need to say another word.

Fifty people armed with pestles and hoes, clubs and machetes, swooped down on Bertignac. The nurses who had accompanied him were long gone, abandoning their medical supplies. The shelter where he stood was in the middle of the village, in the middle of a courtyard the size of a football field. Bertignac put his head down and charged straight ahead. The women grabbed at his hair, almost managing to scalp him several times, but were more skillful wielding the pestles; he took one hard blow to the ankle, fell, rolled, and took another few blows to the back, but managed to get up before the men reached him. Terrified, he ran toward a group of huts behind which rose the safe haven of the forest, and disappeared.

💚

Not far from the village of Donenkeng lay the Bafia Health Center, headquarters of the subdivision's medical service. Unless the clinic was open, not many people were on the health center grounds. Nine people lived there full time: Dr. Monier and his spouse, two nurses on call, and five natives who filled various subaltern functions. The uprising in Donenkeng broke out when the first were absent, back in France for their administrative leave. When the others heard about the ruckus in Donenkeng, they took to their heels and fled. Consequently, the insurgents found no one there.

At dawn, more than two hundred natives had surrounded the grounds of the health center. By word of mouth and tom-toms, the incident the night before in Donenkeng had become a regional problem. People from the farthest villages came to fill the ranks of the insurgents. Young people for the most part, they stood firmly behind Abouem, the younger son of the deceased chief, and obeyed him. They were singing and performing war dances nonstop.

As soon as they heard the uproar, most of the Europeans posted to the region raced to Chief Administrator Cournarie's residence. The health auxiliaries managed to escape the villages where they'd been seeing patients, and took refuge in this sanctuary, which the rioters were still hesitant to attack. All were accounted for, except François Bertignac— no one had any idea what had happened to him. Several nurses and native aides had followed their white chiefs into hiding, but most had scattered, disappearing back into nature. Since only Blacks could now travel freely, a *boy* was sent to Yaoundé to inform Dr. Jamot.

❧

The rain had stopped. Damienne Bourdin's feet were bruised and battered from having walked all the way from Ayos to Yaoundé, where Dr. Jamot was waiting for her. The native *boy* who had been sent to fetch her had toes as muddy as the young woman's boots, yet she hadn't heard him complain, not once, along the trail through the forest. He usually spoke some vernacular, true, but his French was good enough; he'd even served as interpreter when they'd needed to negotiate with the people of Awaé to allow a white woman to spend the night in their village.

Damienne had only been in Cameroon for two weeks, and she was already resigned to covering more than a hundred kilometers on foot. Her boat had disembarked on November 27, 1929. When she presented herself at Dr. Eugène Jamot's offices, he informed her she would be posted to the health services in Sangmélima. First, she would go to the Instructional Center in Ayos for a monthlong training in how to combat sleeping sickness, per official procedure. Despite the omnipresence of manioc at meals, and the determination of the mosquitos, everything started out pretty well. Damienne met other French doctors, including three who, like herself, had come through the École du Pharo—the School of Colonial Medicine run by the Army Health Services in Marseille. Everyone described Jamot as a methodical and meticulous man, sometimes abrupt, who put great stock in formalities. As a result, she was surprised when she was summoned back to see him before the training had concluded.

Arriving at the doctor's residence, she was told he had gone to pay a visit to Paramount Chief Atangana. A *boy* took her backpack, which he stored along the back wall of a clean hut built of wooden planks with whitewashed walls. Then he led her to a rustic bathroom, where two buckets full of murky water awaited her—but this was all done with such kindness that the young woman took heart.

Damienne had barely had time to rest after her bath when someone knocked on her door. Dr. Jamot was waiting for her on the veranda. He made the same impression then as at their first meeting. He was a hulking man, about fifty years old, with a gray mop of hair and matching mustache. After a vigorous handshake, he asked her how she was holding up, and then invited her to follow him. Damienne's feet were still sore, but the idea of walking beside this man whose articles she'd read in journals back in France perked her up.

Outside, the already dreary sun was beginning to set. Jamot and Damienne walked along a neat path bordered by coconut trees, passing scattered huts similar to hers. Nurses, both Black and white, came and went. Natives sitting on the bare veranda floors halted their conversations in Ewondo as Jamot and his colleague passed by. She could feel the respect they had for white doctors. Damienne was flattered, but she knew it was really Jamot they revered; she was just a thirty-year-old doctor, who still had so very much to learn. The main building, which housed the doctor's clinic, his office, and his private apartment, stood at the end of the path. However, Jamot led Damienne down another path opening onto a grassy trail that led down to a freshly graded dirt road. Natives in beautiful white boubous passed them on tired old bikes, no doubt the local elite. Farther down the road was a large cluster of homes, mud-walled huts with roofs covered in straw or woven raffia mats. Along the horizon under an ever-dimming sky, they could see the seven hills of Yaoundé.

Dr. Jamot was worried. His mischievous smile had faded away, and crow's-feet were etched along the corners of his eyes. Wiping his brow, he thanked Damienne for answering his call, and pointed to a recently felled tree trunk, where they sat. Lifting his eyes to the horizon, he spoke in a monotone voice, as if he were addressing the seven hills in the distance:

"Mademoiselle Bourdin, two months ago Monsieur Cournarie, head of the regional administration for Bafia, visited my office. He's an old soldier, a lieutenant in the colonial army, with whom I am on good terms. He was on his way to meet his commanding officer and made a detour to inform me of a curious situation. His men, on a census field mission, had noticed a strange concentration of blind people in several villages in his sector. I admit this information greatly unsettled me, which did not escape the administrator, though I was careful not to share my concerns with him.

"I created a health services subdivision for the preventive mission based in Bafia, which is presently led by Dr. Monier, a young Parisian, twenty-eight years old, trained in Bordeaux. In Bafia, Monier has a staff of ten French health auxiliaries, each of whom leads a mobile unit composed of native nurses. These units crisscross the area, visiting villages to diagnose new cases of sleeping sickness, administer the treatment, gather statistics, and so on. In principle, a mobile unit knows everything about the people living in its villages. Hernias, pregnancies, infant and toddler deaths, everything is noted. It's inconceivable that a sudden increase in blindness would escape the vigilance of the village's medical unit.

"And yet three days before the administrator came to warn me, Dr. Monier paid me the honor of a visit while passing through Yaoundé, staying here with his wife, Madeleine. If their boat arrived in Marseille on schedule, they must already be on their way to Paris, where they will spend the six months of leave the doctor has accrued. Since Cournarie had no reason to go out of his way to spread rumors, my question is, Why didn't Monier say anything to me about this affair? I decided to go myself to inspect the mobile units working in the Bafia sector.

"The first unit I visited was in the village of Mouko. Even before I interviewed the health auxiliary, I saw a woman being led out of a hut by the hand. Through a translator she explained she had lost her sight in the middle of the egusi harvest, about four months prior. The poor woman confided that she'd contracted sleeping sickness and had received regular treatments. She added, in a most grateful voice, that she was thrilled to have been relieved of the debilitating fevers, but she was disappointed that she could no longer sell her egusis and palm kernels. Concerned, I asked to examine the entire population of Mouko. I identified sixteen male and eleven female patients who'd gone blind in circumstances quite similar to the first woman. The health auxiliary confirmed they had all been treated for sleeping sickness following the protocols established by Dr. Monier. Upon my request, the health auxiliary showed me the treatment protocol used, and I thought I would faint.

"I visited all the villages in the region, examined thousands of people, spoke privately with the health auxiliaries, and listened to the native nurses. Each day felt like reliving the same nightmare: the spectacle of all those blind people paraded before me was unbearable. A disaster!

"At this moment, mademoiselle, the subdivision of Bafia has a total of precisely 502 patients with irreversible blindness, and 214 with serious vision impairment. And these numbers are only provisional. The patients in that subdivision were exposed, over a long period of time, to a high dose of tryparsamide, in complete disregard of the treatment protocol I established and that all doctors working for the mission are obligated to follow. And Dr. Monier is not here to explain the liberties he took with the guidelines . . ."

Dr. Jamot paused as a group of eight locals, all barefoot, recognized him and approached. The five women had on simple dresses barely covering their full breasts, and two of the men were bare chested, wearing only a pair of shorts held up with a bit of vine tied around their waists. Smiling as widely as possible, and making deferential gestures, they greeted Dr. Jamot and Damienne, then surrounded them. The locals called them *dokitas*, probably an adaptation of the word "doctor." The one man who wore a shirt spoke a serviceable French; he said they were returning from evening prayers at the Catholic church and he advised the white doctors not to linger as night fell because, he insisted, "the place is infested with witch doctors who will soon be coming out to battle in the coconut trees, as usual." Damienne momentarily thought he was joking, but no, the man was serious. When the group went on its way, Dr. Jamot continued his story.

"Henri Monier went into the field with the passion of his twenty-six years," he went on. "In 1927, he inherited a subdivision where the contagion rate was among the highest in the country. Based on what I learned from his colleagues, Monier encountered marked resistance to the usual treatment among some of his patients. So he began his own experiments, and eventually decided to prescribe a triple dose of tryparsamide to all the patients in the subdivision. That went on for two years. Unfortunately, Monier, whose judgment was clouded by pride and a thirst for recognition, failed to consider the properties of tryparsamide. It's derived from arsenic, which, as everyone knows, is toxic. Even when administered following proper guidelines, tryparsamide can cause optic neuritis in humans. The population doesn't need to know this, but with normal dosages, one expects to find one or two cases of blindness per hundred patients in each subdivision. But in this case . . .

"The administrative authorities have already claimed jurisdiction over the affair. I was summoned. Now Commissioner Marchand is awaiting my report, which he will send to Minister Maginot. You must know that the preventive mission doesn't lack enemies within the administration. Our budgets and autonomy, conferred by ministerial decree, don't make us popular. A scandal is inevitable. And I can already hear detractors calling for my head. But that's not my primary concern.

"Since I've been in Africa, I've found the people to be welcoming overall. Yet all the natives I've come to know in Chad, Congo, and Cameroon are not just superstitious, but mythomaniacal. They see evil everywhere! I had to go through interminable palavers just to convince them that taking blood samples wasn't a way to bewitch people. The first spinal fluid sample I took ended in me being chased out of Deng

Deng. These Africans will happily swallow all the syrups and tall tales you serve up, but as soon as you trim one of their nails, they accuse you of witchcraft, and that's the end of their friendliness. They think Western medicine is a ritual forcibly imposed on Black people. Despite the investment of logistical and human resources in health campaigns, despite the dedication of the hundreds of doctors, nurses, and pharmacists patrolling the African countryside, a good half of the people on this continent still have never seen a syringe. After such a hard-fought struggle, if the other half had any reason to doubt our medicine, the natives would desert the health centers. So seven hundred blind people all at once in a small district is a bomb waiting to go off. In more than one way. It's possible, maybe even probable, that the suspicion will spread beyond the medical field. Since Africans are capable of logical thought, the rejection of doctors could quickly blow up into a rejection of the White Man altogether. The repercussions would be felt in all of the colonies. It would be a catastrophe.

"Thankfully, I didn't notice anything alarming on my inspection tour. No perceptible animosity in the region, because the people hadn't yet made a connection between the growing number of cases of blindness and the injections. Still, that didn't make me any less worried. Crossing through villages, surrounded by Negroes with gleaming muscles, I kept my eyes peeled. I paid close attention to people's attitudes and gestures everywhere I went. In my mind, always the same concern: How would they react if they realized that the blindness of their fellows resulted from those big needles the white men living among them shoved into their skin day after day? We had reason to fear the worst. I was very anxious on my tour, but I couldn't let anyone see it. Those staying in the field, Europeans and even Black nurses from other parts of the country, didn't need me to share my fears with them—especially since it wasn't impossible that the situation would remain calm in the villages and that the scandal might be contained within the administrative sphere. So I kept my composure, at least in appearance, despite the alarming numbers I gathered as I went along.

"My tour lasted a whole month, and when I returned to Yaoundé three weeks ago, I was alone to face an administrative machine thirsty for revenge and eager to take over my organization. Dr. Monier, the principal at fault, was already far away, and it will be six months before we can hope to receive a detailed report from him. I was rereading my own report the other day when I learned of the uprising in Donenkeng, that they'd surrounded the health center in Bafia. My worst fears had finally come to pass.

"Today, I am a shattered man. Beyond what is at stake in terms of health and politics, this revolt poses a very concrete problem for me: it endangers the lives of some fifty of my colleagues spread out around Bafia. As the head of the Permanent Mission for the Prevention of Sleeping Sickness, I am responsible for the safety of my agents. I know everything about each of them, their careers, their goals, their families. These are young men from all over France who haven't set foot back home in four or five years, have left wives and children behind. And there are dedicated natives who have braved innumerable dangers in the pursuit of scientific knowledge, and now carry the hopes of their country's future on their shoulders. Here in Africa, a communications network is at its most embryonic state, but somehow news spreads faster here than anywhere else. The very same day that the people of Donenkeng rose up, news of their anger reached all sixteen other villages in the Bafia subdivision, a mixture of fact and misinformation. The entire zone is now on alert, and any man of the white race is in danger there.

"But the person whose safety is my greatest concern is a native woman. Edoa, a young woman, about twenty years old. She's a nurse. After completing a course at the Instructional Center in Ayos, she's been working for the past two years alongside Dr. Monier. I last saw her five weeks ago, during my tour. She's intelligent and competent.

Besides the fact that she's the first woman in Cameroon to have pursued an education, and the only one to have become a nurse, Edoa has one other significant trait: she is the niece of Charles Atangana. This Charles Atangana is the chief of the Ewondo tribe and the most influential traditional leader in the country, so that's not insignificant. The city of Yaoundé, where the colonial administration is based, is one small part of his vast territory.

"When I arrived in Cameroon in 1921, Atangana received me in his palace, the greatest and most modern residence in the country, wearing a suit and tie. That's where I met his niece, Edoa. Later, when I set up a school for native nursing assistants in Ayos, Chief Atangana agreed to entrust Edoa to me, so she could be trained there. That shows his open mind; men here don't imagine women holding anything but a hoe or a ladle. At the end of her training, the chief gave a great feast. He invited everyone in Yaoundé, and as his brass band blared—because, yes, he has one—he introduced the new nurse in her white smock. I was there that day. I saw how Edoa is not just her uncle's pride and joy, but a symbol for her whole tribe. And now she's captive somewhere in Bafia. How do you think that will be seen, except as a declaration of war! And a tribal war . . . that's the worst thing that could happen right now, given the tension between natives and whites. If nothing is done, we're rushing headlong into chaos.

"As soon as news of the revolt reached me, I rushed to see Chief Atangana. On the one hand, I was counting on him as an intermediary who could calm down the insurgents. On the other, I hoped that he would temper those in power to prevent reprisals. Atangana is the only man capable of negotiating on an equal footing with both parties, of making High Commissioner Marchand yield, and reasoning with the chiefs in Bafia. And he would certainly have agreed to mediate if his niece weren't trapped between the two camps. Instead, he listened to me politely, surrounded by his notables, and then answered that he was giving me ten days to return his niece. If I failed, he would go to Bafia himself. And not for any palaver. That's when I sent for you, Mademoiselle Bourdin. Since it took three days for you to get here, we have only seven left. And if you consider the five days necessary for the trip there and back—on foot, of course—all you have, really, are two days to find Edoa and secure her freedom. Provided, of course, that you agree to leave tomorrow at first light."

"What?"

"Edoa is a woman of strong character who won't want to abandon her colleagues. I chose you because you are also a woman who wants to make her mark. You must do everything possible to persuade her to come back. For this mission I would have preferred someone tried and true, who knows the terrain, the natives, and their customs. That you are a woman will certainly pose problems. But what's most important is that you can be trusted. As you are newly arrived on this continent, you haven't yet taken sides or gotten caught up in any plot. Am I wrong?"

"Well . . ."

"In any event, you are my only hope. Please accept, I beg you. I've already taken steps to ease your task. This afternoon I went to see Chief Atangana and he agreed to loan me his adjutant, Nama. He speaks French and also several other native languages; he'll be your interpreter. He also knows Edoa, so he can help you find her. I'll also send Ndongo. He's a Pygmy who knows the bush as if he were its maker. You can have total confidence that he will get you there. He doesn't speak a word of French, but that doesn't really matter. He's a smart one and he'll figure out how to communicate through your interpreter. Bourdin, let me be frank: Donenkeng is the closest village to the administrative headquarters and the health center where Dr. Monier's operation is based. To get there, you'll need to pass through a good dozen villages filled with blind people and discontents. Given the current situation, it would perhaps be better for you not to be recognized as a doctor . . ."

II: The Obsessions

They left at dawn.

Before they could consider how to handle whatever they'd find in Bafia, they had to get there. If it went well, that meant two days walking on a machete-made forest trail. There might be other modes of transportation in this country, but Damienne had seen only the train onto which she'd been thrust when she got off the boat, which had taken her from Douala to Yaoundé, the center of Cameroon's colonial administration.

The Pygmy guide walked at a devilish pace. He was a small, withered man who took short, rapid strides. He wore only a loincloth cut from some animal skin, and carried a bag slung over one shoulder. Damienne followed, trying to keep up; her satchel held a clean dress and pencil and paper. Nama brought up the rear, balancing their bag of provisions on his head. He was dressed more decently than the Pygmy, even though he was barefoot. That he carried a machete right behind her back didn't help her concentrate on the jagged stumps that poked out from the ground, threatening to slice through the sole of her boot and stab her tender foot. When you are born in Marseille, you are open to diversity, but tramping through the virgin forest between a Pygmy and an Ewondo just isn't something you can really prepare for.

The huts were all so similar that Damienne felt like they were going around in circles. Nothing but mud walls reinforced with bamboo, capped with roofs of woven raffia held down by bits of wood, and empty gaping holes for doors and windows. Each time they came upon people in front of a hut, Nama would greet them; sometimes the embraces dragged on interminably. The interpreter seemed less concerned by their race against the clock—which was not in their favor—than by being seen in the company of a white nun.

Religious leaders do not pass unnoticed in Africa. People stopped them to offer Damienne eggs, a goat, or a bunch of plantains. As soon as they saw her habit, the natives in Yaoundé were ready to jump to her bidding. The fake sister, impressed by such piety, addressed a silent prayer of gratitude to the first missionaries who had done such thorough work. She regretted, however, that they hadn't thought to tell the Blacks that the White Man was God, for they certainly would have believed them, and it would have made her task much easier. The only one who didn't seem impressed by her habit was the Pygmy guide; that didn't surprise Damienne, who'd learned that Pygmies were the most uncivilized people in Africa. Dr. Jamot's suggestion that she wear a habit showed how much he really understood the African people. Damienne hoped she could use it to her advantage in Bafia where, unlike the Pygmies, most people had received the word of God. Still, they lost precious time as they made their way through the outskirts of Yaoundé, because she had to stop to bless the many co-wives and their children.

It had been an hour since they'd passed the last hut, and Damienne and her companions walked for another hour still before they reached a river's edge. The Pygmy pointed to where they could wade across. On the other side, he set down his packs. Damienne was only too happy for this respite—she'd been dying to ask for one for a while. The Pygmy announced, and Nama translated, that since they were near the end of Chief Atangana's territory, now was the time to protect themselves. He took several amulets from his bag and threaded them on a cord that he tied around his waist. Nama watched him with evident disdain. After tying an identical set around his bicep, he explained that these grigris would make him invisible to his enemies. Then he asked the young woman what sort of grigris she possessed. She showed him her crucifix, which he examined carefully, nodding his head and pursing his lips like an expert. To complete his protection, he swallowed nine seeds from a dried pod. Then he gestured for Damienne to do the same, and she swallowed the mysterious things that her limited education did not allow her to identify. When he held out the seeds to Nama, he just glared—the Pygmy didn't insist. From their resting spot, they still had several hours of walking before they'd reach Bafia, which began on the far side of a much wider river, the Sanaga. Damienne barely had time to re-lace her boots before the Pygmy set off once more.

As for Nama, there was something weighing on his mind. It was clear this white woman put him in the same category as the Pygmy, who couldn't speak French or recite even one letter of the alphabet. It really bothered him to be compared to a Pygmy. Even if he didn't know the bush as well as that primitive aboriginal who served as their guide, Nama knew east from west, and could write his name. Besides, he'd gone on several treks with whites before, sharing their meals, listening to their conversations, and even picking up a few of their expressions. It wasn't for nothing that Chief Atangana had named him head of protocol, responsible, among other things, for greeting visitors at the gate of the palace. It was important that he be given the respect due to his position and that this white woman understand who she was dealing with. Two baobabs farther, he sidled up to her and started a conversation.

"One evening during a gala at the royal palace," he said, "Chief Atangana told me that in Europe there was a ritual called a 'vote,' where people were gathered together and each was given a piece of paper to show which chief they wanted. How palm wine and corn alcohol had flowed at the palace that night!"

Being open minded, Nama was willing to attribute the strange words of his beloved chief to inebriation. Because you don't consult people to find a chief—that's a question settled quickly by ancestral tradition. And when the time comes to replace a hereditary chief who has died, there's never any shortage of dignitaries to organize a secret investiture ritual. Alas, Damienne confirmed that voting was their tradition, and she tried her best to explain the notion of universal suffrage. After a moment of silence, Nama asked if that ritual would be introduced in Africa, as had the liturgy and identification cards; most of all, he wanted to know if everyone would participate, even the Pygmies. The white woman replied that it was essential that the people express themselves on all matters everywhere, even in Africa. But, she stipulated, in the civilized world it was common for second-class citizens to be excluded from the vote; in France, for example, women and Gypsies were not included. That convinced Nama; all they had to do was identify the similarities between Pygmies and Gypsies and they could hold a vote in Cameroon, since the question of women had already been decided on both sides of the sea. He predicted that the electoral ritual and democracy in general were destined to prosper in all the villages of the region, because the winner would be known before the ballots were cast, as a result of the divine powers held by hereditary chiefs. Having thus proved that he knew how to theorize, Nama left the white woman to draw her own conclusions about her two traveling companions.

Damienne decided to speak to Dr. Jamot about Nama, if she made it back from Bafia, because a native with such a gift for small talk could certainly be put to use. In any case, he deserved better than to be a porter for the great Chief Atangana, even if he was the king of Yaoundé and the surrounding area.

❦

Damienne had lost all sense of time when they finally arrived on the shores of the Sanaga, a wide river they couldn't swim across. Happily, there were shacks and fishing pirogues all over. Naked children buzzed around their rag-clad mothers as they spread manioc paste to dry on wide green leaves. The men wore loincloths, short pants, or even trousers, but all were bare chested and barefoot. There were no fish to be seen, but you could smell them; the odor blended with that of the manioc.

When the three travelers appeared, the villagers froze and all eyes converged on the white woman. She wondered if these people hadn't yet been Christianized, but a wave of servile smiles soon reassured her. The translator passed on several of the compliments addressed to her, and the guide accepted the dried fish they were offered. In the group gathered around them, slender, half-naked young girls jumped and danced unselfconsciously, while muscular boys stared intently at the white woman. She basked in their joyful welcome, knowing such honors would likely come to an end before evening fell . . . There, on the other side of the Sanaga, stood the huts of the first village in the subdivision of Bafia.

Damienne couldn't catch her breath until they got out of the pirogue on the other shore. She preferred having her feet on solid ground, even if in Bafia territory, to rocking precariously in a skiff on the choppy waters of the Sanaga. While she was thinking about how to get around the next village of fishermen, Nama recited an impeccable Our Father, and the Pygmy chewed loudly on a dried fish. They couldn't walk through all the villages in the region. Not just because they couldn't be sure of a warm welcome, but because they would lose precious time. Of course, Damienne couldn't count on her companions to understand this last consideration, because she knew that time, for African natives, is infinite, and therefore has no meaning.

Damienne was about to give the Pygmy an order when she saw two burly men coming to meet them. Others stood stock-still on a little rise. Caught at the river's edge, the travelers couldn't retreat. That the natives expressed no joy at seeing a member of the clergy was a bad sign. But they were dressed just like the natives on the other shore. Since they hadn't made any aggressive moves, Damienne walked toward them. She didn't need a translator: the village chief wanted to see her.

Damienne put on a brave face and, with a ball in the pit of her stomach, climbed up the little hill toward the huts. Natives escorted her. Damienne and her companions could feel that they had left Chief Atangana's territory and were now in the district that, for the past two years, had been visited by Dr. Monier's medical teams. They might encounter their first blind people here, and perhaps their first real problems. Damienne's eyes darted first to the Ewondo and then to the Pygmy. Dr. Jamot had assured her that they knew nothing about the affair and, even if they did, that they weren't smart enough to ana-lyze the obvious political interests, much less the underlying doctrinal stakes. At best they were capable of grasping the tribal implications, as long as a spear or a machete were brandished in front of them.

As for Nama, he was quite calm, though he found it strange that the inhabitants of this village weren't celebrating the arrival of a white nun, but he put that down to their ignorance. The Pygmy remained unflappable. The young woman blessed her companions' ignorance: there was no risk of their turning tail and abandoning her to her fate. Since it was essential not to alarm them, she patted a child on the head and smiled at a toothless grandfather as they made their way through the gathered villagers.

A man stood in front of a shelter, his hair disheveled, wearing a long pagne that left one shoulder bare. He was undoubtedly the chief because, without even turning, he summoned four men who'd been standing behind him, wearing only a short pagne knotted around their waists. Nama confirmed for Damienne that he was the village chief. The whole village was gathered around the shelter, most of the children were naked.

Glaring around, the chief imposed silence. Not one bit of what he had to say could be lost, especially since he had the chance to address a white woman. His first tirade was so long and detailed that Damienne didn't at first realize he was speaking French. She still needed a translation. The chief wanted to know why the nurse he'd been promised still hadn't arrived. She relaxed, because his words showed that, though there were clearly health concerns here, the situation wasn't what she feared. She asked for clarification and was told that the village had been abandoned long ago by its nurse.

"At first," said the chief, raising a hand with his fingers splayed like a fan, "they found five of those bewitched people who sleep or tremble nonstop. The white doctors came and gave them injections, but the Black nurse who was supposed to come each week to give them medicine didn't keep his word. At the start he came once a month, then every three months, and then not at all. After that he came only when the white doctors did, for show. The number of bewitched people kept growing, although we burned the bodies of those who died so that their corrupted spirits wouldn't haunt the village. The day before yesterday we burned one more, and there are thirteen others still quarantined in a hut over there, downriver. Among them is a notable it would be a shame to burn, because his fishing nets would go to his only daughter, who married into another village."

"No, none of the bewitched are blind."

"Yes, the big doctor with the ashy mustache came to see them, and we thought he would send a more dependable nurse. But no one has come, and the people are angry."

Damienne stifled a smile. It was no use explaining to the chief that Dr. Jamot had bigger concerns than an abandoned village, but it was interesting to her that there were patients who owed their sight to the negligence of a native nurse, even though that might ultimately cost them their lives. Damienne asked the name of the careless nurse so that she could report him to Dr. Jamot. The chief didn't know his name, people just called him *dokita* because he wore a doctor's uniform. He added that, given his behavior, he was certainly a Yambassa. The chief, proud to have spoken, warned Damienne not to trust anyone from the Yambassa clan, and not to eat anything in their villages that hadn't first been tasted by her Pygmy. The four notables nodded their agreement and added grunts that the translator chose to omit. The chief, Damienne sensed, was certain his complaint would be relayed to the country's highest authorities, because it had been made to a white person. Damienne hastened to confirm that, and quickly bid him farewell before he could insist she perform an act of mercy and visit the patients downriver.

They needed to hurry if they had any hope of getting through two or three villages before nightfall. But as soon as they were out of the village, the Pygmy indicated that if they wanted to make up for lost time, and possibly even get ahead, they should spend the remaining hours of light eating and sleeping beneath a tree, so they could resume at dusk and walk through the night. Damienne was as surprised by his common sense as chagrined at the idea of walking through the bush at night, given how hard it was even in daylight. One hill farther, the Pygmy pointed out a welcoming thicket. Jealous he hadn't had the idea himself, Nama half-heartedly passed on Damienne's compliments.

Tins of sardines from Douarnenez taste different in a school dormitory in Marseille than they do under a shea tree deep in the equatorial forest. Damienne had never eaten anything more delicious, and Nama, who was trying them for the first time, agreed with her: he almost cut his tongue licking the bottom of the tin. Ndongo the Pygmy suspiciously eyed the fish that hadn't come from the river, then carefully threaded grasshoppers onto a bamboo stick and hummed a little song as he grilled them. He offered some grasshoppers to the others, who declined with a shudder. After their meal, Damienne's companions lay on the ground and quickly fell asleep. She had trouble following their example, though she knew it was important to sleep. Despite their snores, her thoughts flew as fast as the setting sun. She recalled taking the Hippocratic oath dressed in her beautiful naval uniform, her mother watching with tears in her eyes. Even her sister and brother-in-law had come to the ceremony, though beneath the smiles and bouquets of flowers, Damienne knew they were boiling with resentment because, just for once, she was center stage.

In every happy family there are seeds of discontent waiting to grow, and someone always arrives who knows just how to make them sprout. When that someone presents himself as a well-educated brother-in-law with impeccable manners, family meals soon become unbearable. From the day her older sister, Josiane, announced her engagement to Vivian, Damienne had distanced herself, and things had only gotten worse after the wedding. She and her sister had been close since childhood. They had gone to the same schools, where, though they wore matching uniforms and shoes, there was no question of mistaking one for the other. No, they were so unalike, people had struggled to believe they were sisters. Their only similarity was size, though there were three years between them. Josiane was shy, studious, and showed talent in math. Damienne was outgoing, quick to quarrel, and had a penchant for languages. Josiane had brown hair, like their father, and no interest in anything other than her schoolbooks. Her younger sister had her mother's blond hair and was interested in everything, perhaps too much. Damienne went to every party, and Josiane missed them all. In their neighborhood, Damienne had a gang of girlfriends; Josiane spent time with only her sister. It was no surprise that Damienne had her first romance six years before her older sister, who was twenty-three the first time a man kissed her. He was the only man she'd ever known; his name was Vivian. He hated Damienne from the start, and with a ferocity that was more upsetting to Damienne since she couldn't remember ever having been unkind to him. He immediately began plotting against her. While always maintaining his unassailable urbane façade, he exaggerated her smallest difficulties and minimized her every success. Of course, given the life Damienne had led in the two years between enrolling in the School of Naval Medicine and defending her thesis, she had provided Vivian with plenty of fodder for his smear campaign. Before then, Damienne had never worried about keeping up with her sister, because there had never been any competition between them. They had always had a genuine sense of complementarity that benefited both of them. All of that was blown to bits after Vivian's arrival. For Damienne, the hardest thing had been to realize that her sister, under her husband's thumb, had also become her most outspoken critic. Josiane, who'd never once criticized her in twenty years of shared life!

Honestly, it wouldn't be easy for anyone to withstand comparison with Josiane. She'd earned her doctorate and was immediately named to a prestigious professorship in mathematics. She lacked all coquetry, dressing like a vestal virgin in every photo that appeared in the paper, which added to her legendary reputation. Even the shyness that had held her back in her youth had become a strong suit: it was interpreted either as introspection or pride. Everyone admired her; she was all their social group talked about. Even their father, who'd had his own reputation before heading off to the war from which he did not return, had been rebaptized: he was no longer Colonel Bourdin, but the father of Professor Josiane Bernardi. Everyone—from local relatives to citizens living abroad—took pride in their connection to Josiane.

As her sister was starting her rapid ascent toward success, Damienne was taking detours that would lead her away from her studies. It was 1925. Damienne was just about to complete her medical degree when she found herself pregnant. The man in question, to whom she was not married, was a poet her age she'd met at the university in Montpellier. His name was Samuel, and he was the most handsome man she'd ever seen. His eyes were aglow with the golden sun of southern France. They'd been seeing each other for more than a year. Several times, she'd gone with him to Sète during midsemester breaks rather than returning to her mother's home in Marseille, where she lived when not in class. There, in Samuel's modest studio apartment or on the warm sands of la Plagette, Damienne had spent the best moments of her life. In addition to love, she and Samuel shared a passion for literature, and for that alone Damienne would have followed him all the way to China. Since adolescence, she'd been obsessed with literature.

Damienne never wondered where she'd caught the bug, but she'd caught it quite young. She always had a book in her hand as a girl, and eventually her love of reading grew into a passion for writing. At fifteen, she wanted nothing more than to be a novelist. But given her grades, she'd been tracked into science courses. She interrupted writing her first novel to study for her baccalaureate exams—she was working toward a diploma in Latin, science, and philosophy. After earning her high school diploma, she came within a hair's breadth of failing out of her prep-school course because, convinced she'd written a masterpiece, she spent all her time typing copies and sending them to editors. The novel was called *My Mother's Lovers*. None of the editors responded enthusiastically. Meanwhile, Damienne had finished a draft of her second novel, which she thought was even better than the first, but it met with a similar fate. Her mother was beside herself, her sister disparaging, and her sister's husband delighted. The first begged Damienne to return to her studies; the others asked how she was, so they could hear for themselves that she still had her head in the clouds. Everyone knew she would fail; clearly, no editor would publish an unknown young woman, however talented she might be, because no one bought novels written by women. Damienne thought that attitude strange in a country where a single woman had received, in less than ten years, the Nobel

Prize in Physics and the Nobel Prize in Chemistry. She especially didn't see how her sister could tell her that she had no chance to make it as a novelist. It just didn't make sense coming from Josiane, a woman who was shattering glass ceilings every day, armed with only her own gray matter. Still, Damienne forgave her each time, convinced the harsh words were not her own but her husband's. Months went by, and the rejection letters piled up.

Attacked on one side and frustrated on the other, Damienne wasted her prep-school year and, in 1920, enrolled in the medical school in Montpellier. Two years later, she was admitted to the School of Naval Medicine, and everything had gone swimmingly until her pregnancy—

A rough hand shook Damienne's shoulder. She jumped. For a moment she thought a terrifying mask loomed down over her. It was night. It took Damienne a moment to pull herself together. The Pygmy motioned that it was time to depart. She had fallen asleep remembering a life that seemed so far removed and abstract.

The first day of their trek had given her hope: Damienne was in Bafia territory and, luckily, still walking free. True—they had two-thirds of the journey ahead of them before they'd reach the site of the revolt. And they'd soon come across villages where the medical teams had been more conscientious and would therefore be full of blind people and malcontents.

Before dawn they passed seven villages. Damienne was at a breaking point: she'd had enough of tripping over tree trunks, shuddering at every unidentified noise, and trying to hold back a cry each time she mistook a vine for a snake. She hadn't washed since they'd left Yaoundé, so she had lost the right to complain about any odor whatsoever, and hygiene was no longer a priority for her. It was imperative that she arrive at Dr. Monier's headquarters before nightfall, and the route ahead was long and perilous. There was just one thing to do: walk. To pass the time, Damienne dove back into her memories . . .

In France, when she realized she was pregnant, she simply disappeared from classes and her social circuit and went to hide in Sète, at Samuel's. The poet was going through a period of self-doubt, unemployed and without a collection of poetry in the works. The lovers' walks they took along the lateral canal grew rarer and lost the air of frivolity that had made her believe that Sète was the most beautiful place in the world and Samuel the best of all lovers. As weeks passed, it became harder for her to understand her partner. He accepted odd jobs that he'd previously deemed below him, and even before you could glimpse the first hint of a round belly, she adjusted to spending her days alone. That's how Damienne plunged back into writing.

❦

Dr. Jamot emerged from his office for a breath of fresh air. Clearly, he was having trouble focusing on his work. He had sacrificed everything for this mission.

At the end of the war, when he decided to dedicate himself to fighting sleeping sickness, he left everything behind to set up a team in Africa. At first, the team was just five European assistants and five native porters. After several adventures in Chad and in the Congo, he had settled in Cameroon. In the past ten years, no one had crossed the country more times than he and his team. They'd been everywhere in the bush. All along the Nyong and Mbam Rivers, to villages lost deep in the Lobéké forest, where no native had ever seen a white man; up the Logone and Shari Rivers; and then south, where they got lost a hundred times only to have the Pygmies find them every time and lead them back to Kribi or Lolodorf. The first two years, Dr. Jamot examined almost five hundred thousand people. Everywhere it was the same awful situation: on average, three in ten natives were infected with sleeping sickness. He had encountered extreme cases where two-thirds of a village were infected, as in Abong-Mbang. Sleeping sickness and malaria were causing such damage that, if nothing were done, the population of Cameroon would be cut in half every fifty years. Jamot had thrown himself into the fight. After trying several different treatments, he finally developed an effective strategy for combating sleeping sickness. He administered a combination that included atoxyl or tryparsamide. He carefully tested this method, which was then taught to all newly arrived doctors at the Instructional Center in Ayos. Armed with promising results, he met with Monsieur Perrier, the minister of the colonies, to convince him to create a new, well-funded administrative unit dedicated to the eradication of the terrible disease. And so the Permanent Mission for the Prevention of Sleeping Sickness was born in 1926. Ten doctors and twenty health auxiliaries from France had been sent to support the mission. Jamot divided the territory of Cameroon into seven subdivisions; then, having recruited and trained some hundred native nurses, he sent his teams into the fray, armed with microscopes and medicine. They went from village to village and examined everyone; those who were deemed infected were treated according to the protocol, which included very specific dosing guidelines. Less than two years after the launch of the campaign, they'd recorded a clear decline in the rates of contamination. Both Jamot's team and the mission's budget had grown over the years.

Now sleeping sickness was on the brink of being vanquished in Cameroon. There were small pockets of contamination here and there, and Jamot hoped the blunder in Bafia wouldn't compromise the eradication process. The mission must continue until the last patient was cured. Since sleeping sickness is very contagious, any interruption in the prevention campaign could set Cameroon back ten years or more.

And that, Jamot couldn't accept. The mission was his life. The blunder had hit him hard, but he had no intention of giving up, even if he was no longer optimistic. He would have liked to rush off himself to settle the situation with Edoa, but he restrained himself. He was easily recognizable, and the living incarnation of the White Man's medicine to the natives. His presence in the middle of the rebellion might add flames to the fire. He needed someone neutral, like Damienne Bourdin, completely unknown and a woman to boot. And yet Jamot hadn't slept at all since she left for Bafia—he knew the risks she would face . . .

🦋

Experts in the craniology of aboriginal tribes determined an exact series of categories into which individuals could be placed according to the shape of their head. The best of these learned men had, in the previous century, written books proving the existence of tribes in Africa practicing cannibalism not as some mystical ritual, but as a regular part of their diet. Damienne had learned so much about African mores from these experts that she was shocked to not yet have seen a single person with a bone through their nose. Perhaps, she thought, with basic literacy and evangelizing, a few rudiments of nutrition, and love for your fellow man, they had succeeded in lightening the local menu, and perhaps her fear of ending up on a spit amounted to hypochondria. But one glance at the Pygmy guide and she was back on high alert; with those glowing eyes and teeth filed into sharp points he looked ready to chew on a calf, with no regard for provenance. After all, the last century had ended only thirty years ago, and dietary habits are always the most persistent. Prudence.

Damienne had put to rest her thoughts of avoiding villages by going through the forest, realizing that even with a Pygmy guide it would be more than risky, and still wouldn't foreclose the possibility of an inopportune encounter. The simplest way was to stay on as direct a path as possible, and hope that African hospitality, very much in evidence despite recent events, wouldn't fail her. That said, she hoped she wouldn't have to participate in certain aspects of that hospitality, such as long palavers, which, under the circumstances, might thwart their enterprise. So several kilometers farther, she had mixed feelings when she spotted an apparently peaceful village.

The first thing Damienne saw were some young men digging a grave. As soon as they noticed her, they stopped and whispered to each other, and one of them took off toward the village center. Nama greeted them, but no one answered. Two other young men peered out from the bottom of the grave. The young woman was struck by the cold eyes staring at her from mud-smeared faces dripping with sweat—she quickly realized they had a real problem. Nama plastered a diplomatic smile on his lips and walked toward them, but he stopped when the young men bent down to pick up their tools. Silently, they turned to face the strangers, holding their shovels and pickaxes. Damienne's heart was beating so wildly, she was the last to hear the clamor.

Half-naked men, and women wearing only a swath of cloth tied over their breasts, with dirty feet and mops of thick hair, rushed out of their huts. In just a few seconds, the villagers had surrounded them. Damienne was petrified, unable to move, unable to recognize her two companions amid all those Black faces radiating incommensurable hatred. She instinctively made the sign of the cross and fell to her knees, sure that her last hour was upon her. The next moments, before the strange silence that made her lift her head, remain among the most dreadful of her life.

When Damienne opened her eyes, the first thing she saw were shoes—the first she'd seen on a native's feet since leaving Yaoundé. The man wearing them was clearly someone important, and she owed her life to him. The shoes in question were too big, missing their laces, and needed polishing, but Damienne still would have kissed them. He was wearing a magnificent boubou with wide long sleeves. But beneath his chechia, embroidered with the same motifs that adorned the front and the sleeves of his boubou, Damienne found a haughty demeanor that did not reassure her. The man gestured for her to stand. Once on her feet she noticed someone standing behind him, wearing a sort of headdress, a mane concocted of leaves and various feathers. He had the imposing air of a caster of spells, and deserved a second look, but Damienne didn't get the chance, because the man in the boubou began to speak. She looked for her interpreter, who was shoved in her direction. He staggered toward her. With a grimace meant as a smile, a sign of his allegiance, Nama informed Damienne that she was standing before the chief of the Yambassa clan. Then he asked who she was and where she had come from so early in the morning. The young woman from Marseille answered that she was Sister Marie-Damienne from the Congregation of the Holy Union of the Sacred Hearts, on her way to the mission of Father Alphonse Bernhard. She added that she was horrified by her mistreatment. Given how long it took to explain what a nun was, Damienne understood that, if so many infidels remained along the main route, she shouldn't put much faith in the habit she wore. The chief beckoned to a young woman whom he placed next to Damienne—it seemed he wanted to compare the two. Damienne stole a glance at the young native woman: all she could see was her crest of hair and her immense bosom, seemingly designed to nurse all the babies in the universe. She was so poised and had such a curve to her hips that even her cousins must have gotten ideas. Damienne thought that if this worthy Yambassa woman were to win the beauty competition, it could put her in an even worse position. Instinctively she arched her back and raised her breasts. Approving murmurs spread among the notables. Then the chief said that at first she'd been taken for the wife of a doctor, but he now understood she was the wife of a priest, so he would listen to what she had to say after the burial ceremony. At that, the young woman beside Damienne spat on the ground and glared at her with defiant eyes. Damienne tried not to think about what danger she might face if this quarrelsome rival with her crest of hair convinced the chief to let them fight it out—which Damienne feared she clearly wanted to do. Focusing her attention on the chief, she thanked him for the precious time so graciously allowed her and asked him whether—

With an authoritative wave, the chief interrupted the white woman and ordered her to behave appropriately. The interpreter whispered to lower her eyes when speaking to the chief. Having already forgotten what she was worried about, she focused again on his shoes. That pleased the chief, who imagined just what one might get such a submissive white woman to do. He continued in a less aggressive voice. He began by telling the white woman it was up to her to prove her innocence. He explained that there was a rumor that the whites had decided to exterminate the Blacks. Seeing that Damienne was left speechless, he added that the doctors who visited the villages had supposedly received orders to sterilize as many women as possible and leave the men impotent. He confessed that, other than the spirits of his ancestors and the mystical powers of Gam, he usually only believed what he saw for himself. And it was obvious to him that there was a plot against his race, because eight people from the village had gone blind after being injected by the *dokitas*.

With that, the chief turned around and gave an order: two notables emerged from the group and headed off. Turning back to Damienne, he was almost in tears as he told her that his first notable, Ambatinda, whose grave was now ready, had been injected by the white doctors and died. He grew angry and declared that the real reason why people like Damienne were traveling the country was to check that the natives were actually dying, and to see when the whites could take over the newly empty lands.

As he spoke, tempers boiled. Some natives, brandishing fists and hoes, threatened Damienne. The two notables who had disappeared returned leading a group of villagers who were leaning on sticks as they walked. This did nothing to improve the situation.

That's when Damienne saw the first eight blind people of what would come to be known as the Jamot Affair. Two women and six men. They stood awkwardly, eyelids fluttering and pupils unfocused, their dark eyes open wide, hungry for a light that they'd never see again.

Boto, the girl with the crest of hair, was confused. Despite her many supporters, and her undeniable physical advantage, she wasn't certain she'd won the battle. She'd heard a lot about white women, but this was the first she'd seen close up. She glared at her. She had to admit that this white woman had beautiful cat eyes and delicate hands. But if all white women were like her, Boto was sure she wasn't just the most beautiful girl in her village, but in the world. And there was no way she was going to let the chief have any doubts about it. Boto was familiar with the look in the chief's bulging eyes: the only thing on his mind was removing those horrible black pagnes the white woman was wrapped up in, as if she had something to hide. She could make peace with the chief spending some time alone with a virgin—Boto had learned to manage those local rivalries by threatening the other woman alone down by the river—but she wouldn't let some stranger, even a white woman, come and challenge her on her home field and escape without a scratch. Boto was determined to keep the village girls in line. Once everyone had turned toward the unfortunate blind people, Boto had an idea: she leapt forward and slapped the white woman hard.

The blow hit Damienne like a cudgel. She fell, splayed out on the ground before the terrified eyes of her interpreter, then rose, cheek aflame. She'd lost most of her bearings in this waking nightmare—a nightmare she'd had occasionally when safely ensconced in her comfy bed. This time, she couldn't just fly away as she did in her dreams. She was just two steps away from being mobbed when the chief brought everyone back to order with a curt roar. He prattled on for a few minutes, but by the time Nama got ahold of himself (though no one had slapped him) and started translating, Damienne had missed half of what he'd said. The chief pulled one side of his boubou up over his shoulder and calmed everyone down, for the moment, saying that since the witch doctor Teketekete had gotten involved, there was no need to worry about evil spells spread by the injections. He regretted that he'd had the last medical team chased out of his village, and admitted it would have been better to capture them, especially since one was a Tikar. For five long minutes, he leveled insults at the Tikar clan, declaring that marriages between Yambassas and Tikars were suspended, and promising that the first Tikar caught would be punished as an example. Then he ordered Damienne to follow him to the other side of the village, where the sick people under the witch doctor's care were being kept safe from evil doctors. The man wearing the headdress with a mane and feathers, the witch doctor, frantically waved a flyswatter and the crowd split in two to let them pass respectfully through.

Damienne was no longer worried about wasting time visiting the villagers infected with trypanosomiasis. In truth, thoughts of Dr. Jamot's mission had long since vanished from her mind. In that moment, she was concerned only with her own survival, and this forced visit to the sleepers seemed like a blessing, since it gave her time to think.

Once across the village, they took a path off through a manioc field and arrived at a shelter. The crowd had thinned and only two notables and the witch doctor accompanied the chief. Now freed from her rival, Damienne was able to think clearly again. About a dozen people lay on mats of bamboo and raffia. Despite everything Damienne had learned in Ayos about sleeping sickness, the sight made her stomach heave. The chief watched her reaction: there in front of the sufferers, she was held responsible for all the torments that colonial ideology had injected, one might say, into this formerly peaceful village. For these simple people, there was no other way to think of it, because she was white.

A horrible stench surrounded the place, stronger by far than all the particles that contributed to the now-familiar scent of the equatorial forest. The patients had swollen faces and enormous ganglions on their necks. Damienne's professional reflexes kicked in; she moved forward to examine some of the patients, but the witch doctor Teketekete, and his bulging muscles, blocked her way. Waving an index finger adorned with a wooden ring, he admonished the young woman with a calm, authoritative voice; she understood his threats clearly, no need for translation. She resigned herself to observing the patients from outside the shelter. One who was racked by spasms would try to sit up, then fall back, limbs flailing like a marionette. The others were motionless; except for their occasional moans, she'd have thought they were dead. They were in the stage with high fevers and intense joint pain; maybe they were already anemic. With only the great Teketekete's smoky incantations and dubious herbal decoctions, delirium and heart and kidney failure were sure to follow. Death was inevitable. Damienne knew it, and her inability to change the course of the disease made her ashamed.

She jumped at a sharp bark from the chief. Now that she had seen the situation for herself, she would be led to the hut of his last wife, who would go stay with his number four. He promised that she would be called on to explain herself to the court of village notables after Ambatinda's burial and the purification ritual led by the witch doctor himself. He made it clear that she was not to poke her nose outside during the sacred ritual, because women and children were excluded from it by ancient tradition and the usual proscriptions. He deemed it important to remind her that it was up to her and her alone to convince him. He concluded by saying that he wanted to settle this issue before the next day, because he wanted to leave in time for the investiture of the new chief, Abouem, which would take place the day after that.

As soon as he finished speaking, two notables escorted Damienne to a tiny hut with a thatched roof, behind a large compound that, relative to the others, was clearly befitting the village chief. Once she was shut inside, they posted a young man in front of the door and another by the back window. Damienne knew she was being accorded a certain honor, since the hut belonged to one who had recently been the chief's favorite.

She wasn't certain her interpreter, from whom she was now totally cut off, was being accorded the same hospitality. Even if craniology hadn't yet gained traction here, her most fervent desire was that he not be seen to have a head like a Tikar. Suddenly Damienne remembered her Pygmy guide; she wasn't sure when she'd seen him last.

A simple bed frame built from wood and bamboo and a mattress of dried grass that poked out through the jute ticking: that was all she saw in his favorite's hut. The mud walls had cracks large enough that Damienne could keep an eye on the movements of her two jailers. The floor had been smoothed but was still uneven; in one corner there was a hole she hoped wasn't an entrance to some animal's den. She walked toward the door, or rather, the woven mat that took its place. The window was covered with a screen of woven straw. After tossing her bag onto the ground, Damienne sat gingerly on the bed, surprised it didn't fall to pieces beneath her. Feeling an uncomfortable spread of cold beneath her thighs and calves, she jumped up. She inspected the bed, imagining the worst sort of contagious diseases. But after feeling around carefully she realized that it was in fact she who had pissed on her own dress.

Damienne was really looking rough. Just as she was thinking of changing her clothes, the door creaked behind her. A woman came in silently, placed a bowl of food on the ground, and left. The hut filled with a pleasant smell, which sparked the curiosity of the woman trapped within. She edged toward it. There were vegetables, but the delicious smell came from the steaming yellow couscous. She hadn't eaten since the night before and her mouth watered, but Damienne couldn't forget she'd been warned about the Yambassas, and the Pygmy wasn't there to taste the food first, so she kept herself from tearing into it.

A concert of wails outside caught her attention. The burial. Everyone in the village seemed to have gathered around the tomb. Later they'd make the women and children hide inside so they could proceed with the purification ritual. And after that . . . Several minutes went by. Suddenly she saw the guard behind the hut move toward the door. Forgetting how tired she was, so exhausted she would have thought she couldn't even move, she grabbed her bag and dove through the window; the screen split open with a loud crack. Before the young men could rush back around the hut, Damienne had already reached the overgrowth. She heard voices shouting, and the thought that they would soon be on her trail put wings on her feet. She had reason to fear that the chief would allow himself certain privileges if she were caught. And the chief's favorite now had a good reason to be aggressive.

After careening between banana and palm trees, she managed to find a trail that headed down into a dark valley. At the bottom a thin stream snaked beneath the looming trees. Three steps through the water, a few more across mud on the opposite side, and she continued her frantic race. Her veil had flown off, leaving her long blond tresses bouncing along her back. Her dirty habit, which she hadn't had the chance to change, was cumbersome. She had to hold one side up to keep from getting her feet caught up in it, but she couldn't stop to take it off until she was a safe distance from the village.

❧

Nama promised himself never ever to step foot in Yambassa territory again. Even though no one had harmed him, he wouldn't spend time with those people who, not content to merely ignore the French language, actually permitted an assault on a white woman—and a nun to boot! A triple crime. Chief Atangana, who was a believer, certainly wouldn't fail to respond after hearing such a thing. And Nama was intent on telling his paramount chief about the inappropriate behavior he had witnessed, so that the chief would be sure to dedicate several hours to retaliation against the Yambassas when he was next on his way to Bafia. The white sister was kind and Nama hoped she would manage to escape from those bumpkins chasing her. But half the village had abandoned the burial to rush off on the sister's trail, and he was worried about her. Still, one positive point: thanks to the diversion, everyone had stopped paying attention to him, and so all he had to do was turn around and set off along the path back to Yaoundé. If he kept a steady pace, he'd be at Chief Atangana's side before the next day.

💋

Damienne thought about her brother-in-law, Vivian; immediately, her brow wrinkled and she clenched her teeth. Thanks to the combined effects of fear and rage, she leapt over huge tree trunks and when she fell, immediately jumped up again. She rushed through spiny thickets and kept going despite her wounds. Every sound made her worry someone was going to dive out and grab her feet. She must have run for hours before realizing she was lost. Her lungs were on fire and all her muscles screamed for her to stop. Refusing to give in, she staggered from one tree to the next, and finally freed herself from her wimple, cape, and black dress, so that she was left in just her panties and a silk camisole. All that remained of the nun's costume was the wedding band; even the crucifix had flown away with the habit. A few meters farther, she collapsed.

There was a noise behind her. Her pulse raced. Damienne jumped to her feet, ready to run, but a hand grabbed her. She howled. The hand, rough and calloused, clamped down firmly over her mouth, and her assailant spun her around. She started to fight like a woman possessed.

When she realized it was her guide, it took all her wherewithal to keep a shard of self-restraint and refrain from kissing him. The Pygmy let her go and she struggled to catch her breath for several minutes, wheezing loudly, hands pressed on her knees, her hair hanging loose. Then she began to cry. When she finally calmed down enough to rise, she noticed he looked worried. Damienne first thought that they were in some imminent danger, but the intensity of the gaze beneath the

Pygmy's bushy eyebrows and a telltale movement in his crotch told her otherwise: he was not indifferent to the young woman's change of attire. She looked at herself. Her sweat-soaked camisole clung to her breasts, highlighting their sensual curve. A reflex of modesty made her bring her arms together across her stomach, which only made her nipples stand out more. Facing her, his Adam's apple bobbed wildly.

Since she was without her crucifix, the Pygmy took some amulets from his own grigris and made one for the white woman, which he tied around her waist.

Damienne's situation was vastly improved: she had escaped from a horde of Yambassas and now found herself at the mercy of one lascivious Pygmy. That her guide would fantasize about her seemed plausible. But what bothered her was that this primitive man might believe he had any slight chance with her. Damienne had always felt a sense of superiority over the few Blacks she had seen in France. Since being in Africa, that feeling had only grown. She was gratified to see that the natives, for the most part, seemed to share her opinion, and no one seemed bothered by it. She supposed that the concept of racial inequality was a given for people who denigrated each other even more than others denigrated them.

Damienne was upset to have lost Nama, the interpreter, but she was happy to have found the guide Ndongo again, even if she couldn't communicate her instructions to him. Problems just kept piling up, she didn't know what to do. Having returned to his usual calm, he seemed to find everything perfectly normal. After looking at the sky, he hurriedly gathered some vines. Then he bent several spindly bushes growing side by side and, knotting their stems together, created a sort of dome. Next, he attached branches to the sides of the dome, and then he gathered leaves and layered them one over the other, attaching them to the branches. In just a few minutes Damienne saw a little hut take shape. In a whispery voice the Pygmy jabbered something in his dialect and gestured for the white woman to go into the hut. She shook her head. He insisted and, in a flood of words, she managed to pick out the word *mungulu*—he said it each time he pointed at the hut. She began to repeat the word *mungulu* back to the Pygmy, who beamed at her.

As Damienne tried to make him understand that they didn't have time to try his *mungulu*, a raindrop bounced off her nose, followed rapidly by many others. She hurried into the hut just in time to avoid the downpour. The Pygmy followed on her heels. There they stayed, crouched, side by side, thigh against thigh. To escape her fear of being ravished, Damienne sought refuge in her memories.

Motherhood had brought an unimagined sense of satisfaction and a whole lot of unexpected problems. For the first time, she felt that maybe writing wasn't the most important thing in the world. Her little boy looked like his father, and she devoted all of her time to him, leaving her manuscripts to molder. Between nursing, washing diapers, preparing meals, doing dishes, ironing, and other unexpected chores, she didn't have enough time left over to complain about anything. Facing practical problems every day revealed her hidden talents and, even more, the indolence of the man who was supposed to face them with her.

Swallowing her pride, she went to Marseille to ask her mother for money. Her mother told her, in a voice on the verge of tears, that everyone at church knew about her bastard and that she'd been excommunicated, which, of course, cast a taint on the whole family's honor. Damienne listened distractedly. She left feeling that her mother was suggesting she leave her partner and move home with her son.

Twenty-four hours later, Josiane and Vivian knocked at the door of the studio apartment on the rue du Sar—though Damienne had only revealed that address to her mother—arms laden with clothes for the baby and for her, and even some prepared meals. Damienne swallowed her shame at her life choices. Her brother-in-law managed to find some vague words that both praised the young mother's courage and also underscored her frivolity.

The Pygmy stood up. The storm had passed without a single drop coming through the leaves covering the *mungulu*. Ndongo tried to say something to Damienne, but she couldn't make heads or tails of it. She laid her bag on the ground and, bringing her two hands together, mimed to him that she wanted to bathe. He understood and, after looking carefully at the ground, pointed in one direction. The white woman couldn't see why; there were trees all around and nothing like a path. She didn't move. Ndongo sighed; clearly, these city people understood nothing at all. He took her by the hand and led her himself. They went around a network of thorny vines, balanced across a tree trunk to get over a crag, and climbed a hill. At the top of the hill, Damienne could see a river on the other side. She smiled at Ndongo, who welcomed it as a fitting reward. When they reached the riverbank, it didn't occur to him that he should turn away, so she washed herself under his vigilant gaze. He gathered some ferns for her to dry herself with. And, since the nun's outfit had lost its protective properties, she decided to defrock herself once and for all. From the bag, she grabbed a short belted dress, frankly more appropriate for a romantic dinner at the Splendide Hôtel than this trek through the muddy bush that fate had imposed upon her. Not a bit of breeze managed to find its way beneath the trees. Happily, the young woman's underclothes, which she'd washed and put on while still damp, helped her bear the heat.

They set off again and walked along the river for hours.

A new day dawned. Totally disoriented, unable to direct her guide, Damienne just followed him, hoping he would lead her somewhere less savage, or even take her back to Dr. Jamot. She could already imagine the great man's disappointment. The mission he'd entrusted to her, and to which she'd selflessly given her all, had failed before she even made it to Bafia, where Edoa and several other members of Dr. Monier's team were supposedly trapped. As she wandered through the forest, struggling to stay alive, with no way to let Dr. Jamot know of her defeat, precious time was slipping by. Just four more days and the time allotted by Chief Atangana would run out.

At Damienne's side, the guide kept moving ahead placidly, blissfully unaware of the chaos threatening the region. Rather than wasting energy on all those what-ifs that worried his companion, he focused on the essentials: walking with his bag slung over one shoulder and his belt of fetishes, stopping now and then to capture grasshoppers or to pick some buds and pop them into his mouth. Damienne observed him with growing attention. She had already seen that he focused on only three things: his food, his libido, and his safety. Truth be told, most men don't have any obsessions but those, but Damienne was still fascinated by the ease with which the Pygmy focused on his. This practically naked man leading her through the heart of the virgin forest seemed to have a compass in his head. Of course, Damienne suspected he wasn't a gifted conversationalist even if they could speak to each other; he'd never read a book and wasn't interested in existential questions. And yet as Damienne watched him live, she was convinced she'd never met anyone with a keener mind for the issues that mattered most to him. She wanted to inform him of the dangers ahead, rouse him from his implacable bliss, but she didn't dare. In fact, she couldn't, even if she wanted to.

They stopped to rest several times. Damienne was dirtier than ever but didn't even think about another bath—but not for a lack of running water. Drinking from a stream like an animal, lapping at the surface, was no problem for her. In her current state, she'd stopped worrying about the finer points of life. Finding a cherry tree had lifted her mood—and let her stock up on cherries—but exhaustion had overwhelmed her again and she'd abandoned her bag. Several kilometers later, she felt as if her burden was even heavier. When her boots got too hot, she tried to walk barefoot, like her guide, but thorns tore her ankles and calves, and she put them back on. Ndongo led her patiently, and she tried to be worthy of the company of this heaven-sent man. All things considered, she couldn't complain, but the fear of being bit by a tsetse fly kept gnawing at her. Suddenly he stopped and crouched down. Damienne followed suit. Ndongo put a finger to his lips and stared at her; with his other hand he gestured for her to stay put. Then he crawled under some bushes and disappeared.

Damienne opened her ears and tried to listen for suspicious sounds, but all she heard was leaves rustling and birds chirping—sounds that had been with them for hours. It was starting to get dark. Something moved on her left. Calmly, she turned and saw two tortoises, one hiding in its shell. Rather than wondering where the Pygmy was, Damienne let her mind wander, contemplated the play of color on the greenery filtering the rays of the setting sun. Even the tiny mosquitos relentlessly biting her head to toe, so her skin was covered in bumps like a toad's, no longer bothered her. Maybe she'd already lost her mind, because she never once worried about where she would spend the night, nor even about what she'd do if her guide never returned. She'd really needed to stop and rest. She wondered whether her fear of the tsetse fly was rational or if it was one of those things that people worried about for the sake of having something to talk about—like fashion, religion, the accumulation of diplomas, priestly blessings, and other things you can't eat, like democracy, legality, equality for all, tipping, and other lofty ideals that no Pygmy would ever give a hoot about, which were still on the front page of French newspapers. Drifting from one thing to another, Damienne's mind wandered back to her own memories.

Her uncle had found her an internship with a newspaper. Although writing had been Damienne's obsession, she'd never dreamed of being a reporter. Still, so as not to overwhelm her poor mother, she'd given up on her fourth novel, already two-thirds written, to join the press. Maybe she would have stayed if the editor hadn't kept moving her from one department to another, giving her every assignment except writing articles. He'd forced her to attend all the editorial meetings, during which she was expected to sit quietly and suffer through the misplaced criticisms colleagues leveled at the lead story in some other paper the day before; after those critiques came endless debates about how to frame issues for the following day's edition. Six months later she was still doing nothing—she hadn't been paid a cent and had not one byline, but she knew all the sordid details about how to bamboozle people with misinformation, blackmail politicians, and crucify people in the press.

One morning, Damienne decided that her internship was over. She went to the editor in chief to let him know. He greeted her with uncharacteristic enthusiasm and swore that, since no one else was available, he needed her to go to Paris to cover the Coupe de France football championship, where Olympique de Marseille would play Union Sportive Quevillaise the following day. He also wanted a profile of goalie Charles Allé. Damienne thanked him for finally thinking of her and added that she had no intention of wasting one more day in his newsroom. As she left she saw in his eyes that he thought she was mad to turn down so cavalierly an assignment that his most decorated reporters would have begged for.

Instead of going home to face her mother, Damienne rushed straight to Sète where a debonair Samuel awaited. He was more his old self now that he no longer had to push up his sleeves and feed his son—to be honest, he didn't mind that the baby was left with its grandmother. Damienne got back to work. After a month working in peace and quiet, her new manuscript, entitled *Live Happy, Die Young*, was under review by several editors. But self-doubt set in. She was surprised to find that on more than one occasion she regretted not having jumped at the chance to cover the finals for the paper; she imagined her name in a byline on the pages of an important daily paper, respect from all quarters, every door open to her . . .

As her classmates from medical school were being named to their first positions all over France, she was deep in the blues, hidden away in a shed in Sète, having almost forgotten the top grades she'd gotten on her exams. At the same time, her sister was the toast of the town, her praises sung at conferences and in papers, with Vivian prancing like a peacock beside her. Their mother was tearing out her hair. They all agreed: Damienne personified the very worst of Marseille.

One day, there was a knock at the door. Damienne glanced at Samuel, wondering who it was; he shrugged his shoulders. They never dared receive company in their lodgings, and it augured nothing good that someone had come knocking. It was Vivian. He'd come to fetch Damienne, to take her to the charity hospital in Marseille, where her baby had been admitted. She was told nothing more and they sat in silence the whole way there. When she arrived, her sister and mother were leaving the hospital. No, it couldn't be . . .

❦

Silently the Pygmy crawled back toward Damienne and the somber thread of her thoughts was broken.

Ndongo told her what he'd seen. He took her arm and rubbed it so she would understand. Since she continued to stare blankly at him, he told himself he'd need to start at square one with this woman. Finally, he moved back three meters and gestured for her to follow him.

A fat frog on which Damienne had knelt hopped away with a loud croak. The poor girl was about ready to do the same, when Ndongo started moving from tree to tree. She followed his example. Suddenly she heard a human voice, and a European accent. Emerging from the bush, Damienne found herself facing three men who jumped to their feet as one, overcome by unnameable panic. She realized how careless she'd been when she saw that one of them held a machete. Seeing she was white, the three men each swore in their own language and gasped. Damienne was in a tight spot. She realized she'd managed to stumble on a mobile medical unit from the two bags and iconic wooden medical kit lying on the ground. Two native nurses were accompanying a white man, who wouldn't stop wailing that the color of his skin made him a target. Damienne took charge of the situation.

"Dr. Damienne Bourdin, medical officer, second class," she said, holding out her hand.

"Jacques Thouvenin, health auxiliary assigned to Bafia Health Center," her compatriot replied, staring at her intently.

"I'm actually headed to Bafia, myself. I'm to fill in for Dr. Monier."

"Ah?"

"What a relief to have found you here!"

"The pleasure is mine, madame. These are my nurses, Mengue and Abessolo . . . Please, have a seat, here, the trunk is yours."

She didn't wait to be asked twice. The two native nurses wore normal clothes, like Thouvenin; they were amazed at the sight of such a dirty white woman—and a doctor, to boot. But the group was clearly in a situation not unlike her own, even if they hadn't had to disguise themselves as priests.

"I've been racing through the forest for a whole day, and was worried I'd gone in the wrong direction," she said. "But now that you're here, you'll be kind enough to lead me to Bafia."

"I don't know where you're coming from, madame, and I applaud your courage in facing the forest alone in these troubled times. Keep going in this direction and in less than two hours you will be in Bafia, since you are intent on heading there. But please don't hold it against me if I don't accompany you, because I'm doing my best to get as far away as possible from that place. I hope to have crossed the Mbam River or the Sanaga before daybreak. And if the reason that caused you to leave the main track isn't the same that is hurrying me, well, you have two reasons to follow my example."

"What exactly is going on in the Bafia Health Center?"

"First off, it no longer exists; it was burned to the ground yesterday. I saw the rioters, and I can tell you that no angrier natives have been seen since the Char Bouba war. If it's true you are to take charge of operations during Dr. Monier's absence, well, you are my boss, and I can't stop you. But you will regret it, believe me, if you don't listen to a man who prides himself on being well informed."

"I'm listening."

"I was twenty-seven in 1921 when l left Cherbourg and my native Brittany, which I hope to see again one day. After a few misadventures here and there, I found myself in Cameroon. I'd been living in the area for a while before they formed this subsection of the campaign. In fact, I first served two years in the public works department. We built the trail from Yaoundé to Bafia, and also several administrative buildings. I became a health auxiliary in 1924 because Dr. Deumié, who'd arrived to establish the new administrative subdivision, wanted to employ expatriates like myself who already knew the area. From the beginning, I was given charge of Gouife and Bitang, villages which were still under my charge until yesterday, and where, until then, I'd only ever seen people smiling or sick.

"You may not have occasion to verify this yourself, given the circumstances, but the people of this region tend to be calm, indifferent, even. You can see it in their faces. They all have round cheeks, at least when they're healthy, and not because they eat so much corn couscous. They are also extremely gullible—a trait that has facilitated a good number of things—and the few priests who venture this far will confirm that you can put your faith in the word of a Bafia, and even a Yambassa. Although they're chock full of superstitions—they worship the tortoise and are convinced the tarantula has magical powers—they would never think to contradict a white man much less to attack one, unless they felt they were in grave danger. I should know: several times I've spent a whole month in one of my villages, just for the joy of living there, and emerged unscathed from certain little situations that would've led to a marital drama in other places. I continued to provide medical care and live in the same villages while working first for Dr. Sanner, who replaced Deumié, and then under Dr. Monier, who took over the subdivision in 1927.

"As with his predecessors, my collaboration with Dr. Monier was based on absolute loyalty. Although I'm not from the tightly knit medical world and wasn't inspired by a genuine calling, I focused on my work and followed protocols to the letter. I still remember when Monier brought us together in the health center, the other health auxiliaries and me, to train us in the new treatment protocol he'd developed. It was a sunny afternoon in January 1928. I remember it clearly because Madame Monier, who had joined her husband in Africa, made the most delicious grilled doe I've ever had the privilege of drooling over. To pass the time, we each told about our life among the natives in the villages. No one even mentioned the dose of tryparsamide. And yet decorated health auxiliaries with diplomas earned back in France were there—and they'd already gone through several trainings with Doctors Jamot and de Marqueissac. In their defense, they were almost all military officers or retired soldiers. The medical team was in fact a militia that, first and foremost, obeyed the orders of a demanding superior officer. The next day, after the barbecue, we went back to our units, briefed our nurses, and from then on, it was a triple dose—full steam ahead.

"Obviously, we were thrilled when this treatment bore its first fruit. To see those who'd been given up for dead revive and resume their normal activities, that was huge! We shared that moment of glory with the head of our subdivision. Personally, I was welcomed like a hero in Bitang: the notables organized a celebration to thank me for bringing one member of their community back to life. That's why it's hard for me to condemn Monier. When the first two cases of blindness appeared in my sector, I ignored them. But a week later I found myself with eleven cases of blindness—me, a simple health auxiliary—and shared my concerns with Le Toullec, who's the number two in the subdivision. When he admitted that he'd already encountered sixteen cases in his sector, I sensed the scale of the blunder. We'd all met when getting supplies at the center, but the question was never raised. No one was fooled, though, you could see it in their eyes. There's no way Dr. Monier didn't know, because he was personally in charge of Donenkeng, the village closest to the health center. After Monier's departure, things got more and more tense, people started grumbling, and so there we all were, perched on a volcano, when Dr. Jamot came through on his tour and we were finally able to discuss the situation with him. I confess I was almost ready to desert my post when I learned how many cases of blindness there were. At least forty in each village, and one in every family! The folks in the bush just kept on smiling at us, even after such a disaster, which almost convinced me that the Bafias were totally apathetic. Then the chief of Donenkeng and his son died, both on the same day. That's how the revolt started, led by a fellow named Abouem; he's the one who ordered the burning of the health center.

"The worst is perhaps yet to come, because as we speak, the local dignitaries are coming to Donenkeng for the investiture of that same Abouem. That man, barely thirty years old, is the only son of the former chief, and now he'll succeed his father. In my humble opinion, it won't be easy to make him see reason. Yet he knows how to read, he's been baptized and speaks French fluently. Sometimes he even wears a jacket and tie. The young men of all the clans see him as their role model.

"Preparations for the coronation, an important ceremony for the natives, happily distracted our captors; when they let down their guard, my companions and I escaped. That's why we're in such a rush. Once that Abouem has thrown gas on the fire, we want to be a safe distance away, and hear by word of mouth what happens at the meeting of the chiefs. Cournarie, the colonial administrator, was supposed to play an active part in tomorrow's ceremonies, since his duties include the oversight of palavers and the naming of traditional chiefs. I know he's brave; during the war he fought with a regiment of dragoons and then a battalion of infantry, and he speaks proudly of having escaped gassing twice. But I hope this time he will find the courage to flee from his responsibilities, because for the past week, these Bafias are no longer what they were. I'm normally on excellent terms with the chief and notables of Gouife, a village with the most welcoming natives in the world. I spent so much time there that I know everyone by name and have even learned a few words in Bafia from the young men—words that entertain girls and annoy grandmothers when they hear them in my accent. Yet now I'd prefer to be caught in a hostile village than seek asylum in Gouife—I saw men from there among the rioters."

"Your behavior is certainly understandable, no one could blame you. Thank you for informing me of the situation. Do you happen to know a nurse named Edoa, and do you have any news of her?"

"Edoa? Everyone knows Edoa! She's the only female nurse working for the mission. An amazing woman. Now that you mention it, I realize I didn't see her among those of us who sought refuge at the administrator Cournarie's home. Maybe she's among the natives who've cut ties with the group . . . We must leave now. We're planning on going to the Mbam River and finding a place we can swim across. If we succeed, we'll try to make it to the train line. What are your plans?"

"I'm too tired to follow you now. Since you assure me that Cournarie's residence is near, I'll go there. Now that night has fallen, I may have an opportunity to get in. Good luck to you."

The Pygmy, who had stayed clinging to a tree when Damienne rushed toward the fugitives, reappeared as soon as they had left. It was clear now that despite the surprising turn of events, the strange little man had remained focused on getting to their initial destination and had led the white woman to the outskirts of Bafia. All that remained was to enter the town and find the administrator's residence.

Meeting Thouvenin had been useful, though it had also shaken Damienne from the state of semipeaceful calm she'd found by modeling her behavior on the Pygmy's. She had almost succeeded in driving Dr. Jamot's mission from her head before, but as they approached their goal, Damienne's obsession with success—and her fear of failure—had returned. The pride she felt at having reached her destination was overshadowed by the fear of having all of it come to naught if no one in the administrator's residence could put her on Edoa's trail. Ndongo began speaking quite casually, without any gestures, as if his particular dialect was understood all around the world. Damienne followed him. As they walked toward Bafia, her thoughts returned to her baby, and her eyes filled with tears. Once again, she forgot her present circumstances.

Nothing so painful had ever happened to her. One month after his burial, she still hadn't regained the ability to speak—but no one seemed to notice because no one wanted to speak with her anymore anyway. The loss of her baby had plunged Damienne into a kind of contemplative life, a vegetative state one might even say. As long as she remained at the bottom of that hole, the pain was bearable. She had no allies, not even Samuel; she hadn't seen him since. As far as anyone was concerned, they couldn't expect anything more from her. It all seemed so cut and dried that, after a while, Damienne started to notice a few small signs of indulgence on the part of her three closest relatives. The sort of indulgences you might accord to the feeble minded, or the dying.

That was the final blow. Damienne wrested herself from depression and went to the medical school to plead her case. No one there had expected to see her again—it had been two years since she'd left. The dean examined her file and all the little notations—about how conscientious she was, how well she did in oral exams, in practicums, and in her internship. How had she thrown away such potential, he railed! What had gotten into her head! He paced in his office, quite beside himself. Damienne sat meekly and swallowed down all his reprimands without any attempt to defend herself. Finally, the dean turned, pointed a finger at her, and said he would give her one last chance. When, a year later, Damienne announced at a family dinner the date of her doctoral defense, no one believed her. And yet it took place and was a clear success. Immediately afterward, Damienne began an internship at the School of Colonial Medicine in Marseille, at the Pharo, where she spent another eight months studying tropical field medicine. This time, she barely made it through, graduating twenty-ninth in a class of forty, and so she had no choice but to join a regiment of the colonial infantry, which informed her of her posting to Cameroon. On November 3, 1929, she boarded a boat bound for Africa.

Damienne remembered every moment of the last week waiting for the cargo ship the *Amérique* to be readied for departure; the farewell dinner that Josiane and Vivian made sure to host at the Splendide Hôtel; the anchor lifting in the port of Marseille, with all the wives and fiancées standing on the quay, crying, waving handkerchiefs, and watching the man of their life sail away. Well, at least Damienne didn't have to bear any long goodbyes. Then three endless weeks at sea, and finally her arrival in Douala. There, the nonstop rain and suffocating heat. All those villages filled with almost-naked natives she saw from the train chugging toward Yaoundé; the packages and poultry passed back and forth through the windows at each stop. Then there were long, unexplained stops in the middle of nowhere. The waves of cold sweat that drenched her when she saw a crowd of Negroes rush from the forest and race toward the train, before realizing they were only coming to look at the locomotive. Finally, Yaoundé. Her meeting with Dr. Jamot. Life in the dormitory at the Instructional Center in Ayos, under the direction of the chief medical officer, Henri de Marqueissac, along with other former students of the Pharo in Marseille or the School of Naval

Medicine in Bordeaux—including some who'd come with their wives, who were temporarily lodged in a village along the river under the watchful eye of a native chief. And then the request from Dr. Jamot . . .

And now here she was, walking into the first clearings around Bafia.

❧

Not a soul in sight as they emerged from the bush. Damienne took her guide's hand and rubbed it on her arm, trying to signal she wanted to find someone of her own race. Miming the gesture of pulling down the brim of a kepi over her brow completed the description. The Pygmy, thrilled to see she was able to learn something, immediately pointed in one direction.

The pair crept into a town that seemed straight from a book of witch-craft. There was something sinister about the place, with huts along both sides of the trail. The trail climbed up. Trees shuddered. A heavy smell of fruit hung in the air. The blinking of hundreds of fireflies hidden in the tall grass seemed to Damienne like so many eyes reproaching her for being one of those responsible for the blindness. A hoot made her jump and she cried out—it sounded like a death knell. She realized how terrified she was, overcome by the fear of seeing hate-filled Black faces burst from the huts. Cracks in the mud walls revealed the glow of fires still smoldering inside. Nary the shadow of a person, but from time to time a snore.

She assured herself she hadn't cried out so loudly, or maybe she hadn't made any noise at all, because her guide kept walking ahead as if nothing had happened. But the incident in the Yambassa village had left deep scars on Damienne, scars that called into doubt her ability to have a career in Africa unless she got ahold of herself and quickly. Josiane and Vivian were probably sound asleep in a nice clean bed—that is, unless they'd gone out for dinner in a fancy restaurant. They probably imagined Damienne bored out of her mind in a ramshackle dispensary in Akonolinga or giving shots to lepers in Eséka; giving quinine to patients with malaria or putting

Mercurochrome on children with ringworm or yaws. She was sure they couldn't imagine how much worse it actually was.

Exhausted, Damienne still kept walking, driven only by the fear of failing in Africa too. Everything she'd suffered through in her family made it impossible to imagine a return to the status quo, which would only prove her detractors right. The backhanded compliments at her graduation, the insincere encouragements to find a real job, the phony compliments about how she'd finally come to her senses . . . That family hostility was exactly what she needed to spur herself on; it would be unfair if her story ended with her disappearance, leaving the others safe in the comfort of home telling future generations about their thoughtless, self-centered aunt. Her situation was certainly less than enviable, and Damienne still wondered how she'd get out of it, but one thought remained at the front of her mind: she had to go back to France and become what she'd always wanted to be, a novelist. She'd readily admit she hadn't been the best mother, but she refused to give up on her dream.

For the moment she needed to focus on her first priority: finding Edoa—nurse and Ewondo princess—and bringing her back to her community safely. She had to find her in the next twenty-four hours or her mission would fail. And that would be one failure too many for Damienne.

She wondered if Administrator Cournarie's house was being watched. Following her guide to the top of the hill, she knew she had to find out before giving up. To bolster her courage, she told herself if the preparations for the coronation of the future chief of Donenkeng had allowed three men to escape in broad daylight, it had to be easier for one woman to sneak into the grounds at night.

Before seeing the residence, Damienne knew she was on the right path; this was the first time since Yaoundé she'd seen the glow of lights at night. But she wasn't sure whether the light was coming from inside the house or from fires the rebels had lit all around it to discourage anyone from escaping. She couldn't risk going farther without being certain. She suggested to the Pygmy that he go ahead, and he took the precaution of having her hide in a bush before he disappeared. It took him a good fifteen minutes to come back. She couldn't make heads or tails of his report; not only was he whispering lightning speed in his own hermetic language, it was also so dark that she could barely make out the whites of his eyes. All Damienne understood was that, whatever happened between then and dawn, she must never lose sight of the Pygmy. Since she still didn't know if there were guards around the residence, she took him by the hand and pulled him toward the hill—if he refused to go, she'd know. He didn't protest.

The building was big, bigger even than Dr. Jamot's office and residence. In the dark it looked like it had a peaked roof covered with metal sheets or tiles. There were many wide windows, all closed tight; light, probably from hurricane or gas lamps, filtered out through slits in the shutters. She could just make out two huts on either side of the building. The main house rose up in the center of a wide, treeless yard. Fires burned outside. Damienne and Ndongo hid in a shadowy corner, just beyond the perimeter of the residence. From where she crouched, she saw three bonfires along the edge of the courtyard; maybe there were others behind the house. The Pygmy stretched out his arm and Damienne, looking closely, saw people lying around the fires. Were they sleeping? The door to the main house was straight ahead.

To reach Colonial Administrator Cournarie on the night of December 14, 1929, she would need to cross an open area of some hundred meters, through a courtyard surrounded by natives on high alert. She had to hope that they were asleep, and pray to God that the door would be opened before they woke.

Without thinking twice, Damienne ordered the Pygmy to go first. He stood up and clambered down the trail, and for a moment, she lost sight of him. He reappeared on the edge of the property and was walking calm as could be across the courtyard toward the house. Hidden in the dark, Damienne nervously watched the guards, who lay on the ground as Ndongo passed only a few meters away. When she thought she saw one rousing, she clamped both hands over her mouth. The following seconds were unbearable, but nothing happened. He reached the veranda, and she lost sight of him again. Then Damienne realized he was now facing even greater danger, because he had certainly been seen by the people inside. If she didn't join him immediately, anything could happen.

Damienne started, keeping to the shadows. Without rushing, but not without fear, she passed within five steps of a group spread out on the ground snoring so loudly they drowned out the crickets. Flames sent shadows dancing over their sooty bodies. In the distance she saw the Pygmy bend down and pick something up. A burning log crackled. Damienne kept moving; she was about ten meters from the porch when she heard the distinctive click of a dead bolt. Instinctively, Damienne leapt forward.

By the time the door opened completely, she was on the veranda and had the Pygmy pinned to the ground. She felt a comforting arm grasp her shoulder, encouraging her to stand. Before rushing into the house, she turned and caught sight of many silhouettes now standing around the bonfires. The door slammed shut on this scene out of Dante's *Inferno*.

While a redheaded man fastened the door tight, a man with round glasses took aim with a rifle balanced on his knee. Ndongo looked hungrily at the two enormous beetles he'd caught on the veranda. There were four people in the living room, including one Black man. They offered Damienne a chair and pretended not to see the Pygmy, who took no offense. The man with glasses introduced himself as Pierre Charles Cournarie—and then the questions flew.

First, Damienne wanted to know the time—it was 9:48 p.m. She looked at Cournarie; he was about thirty and rather good looking, though haggard and disheveled—he clearly hadn't shaved for a few days. Damienne had imagined the chief administrator of the subdivision as an old administrative hack from the metropole who'd somehow ended up in Africa, where the colonial cap and mustache identified members of the administrative elite. Here she found herself facing a man about her own age. She gave her own name and rank, and told the story of her journey, which needed no embellishments to captivate her audience. However, she was careful not to tell the whole truth about her mission. The administrator seemed convinced. Cournarie ordered the Black man to show Damienne somewhere she could rest, and returned to his post by a window, keeping watch alongside the redhead and the other man.

The Black man, Bidias, walked ahead of Damienne and told her, in passable French, that there were no more beds. He hoped she would make do with the pillow and mat he unrolled at the end of a dark hallway. With the seriousness of a bailiff he confided to her that since the number of occupants had just risen to twenty-eight, if you counted the Pygmy, they needed seven people to escape for the rest to be able to sleep three to a bed. He was still talking as she passed out cold on the mat.

🌿

Dr. Jamot set off for Efoulan, the neighborhood where Chief Charles Atangana's palace was located. It was clear by his face he was having a bad day. He'd just learned that Nama, the interpreter accompanying his envoy to Bafia, had returned to his chief, all alone. The situation was dire. Ten years of superhuman effort were about to go up in smoke. Jamot replied mechanically to a chorus of greetings, without even glancing at the adoring natives. He was haunted by a vision of the Pygmy Ndongo also returning alone, which would mean the worst for Damienne. As if the hundreds of blind people, the revolt, and the inevitable tribal war weren't enough, now he'd have Bourdin on his conscience too. He became irritated just thinking about the thousand administrative forms he'd need to fill out, and all the traps they held. Jamot had no illusions: the blunder would fall on his shoulders and his name would forevermore be associated with the scandal in Bafia. His reputation would be tainted. For the hundredth time, he cursed Henri Monier and wondered if it would do any good to make him confess. Maybe one day the truth would come out, but he had more-urgent worries on his mind: he needed to convince Chief Atangana to take him to Bafia. He was sure he could be useful there. And if he was part of the entourage of the paramount chief of the Ewondo, he'd be safe. He plastered a smile on his face and picked up his pace.

Damienne wasn't among the first to wake the next morning. And when she did, she was starving. For the past twenty-four hours, she'd eaten nothing but grasshoppers and buds. She hoped she wouldn't have to eat beetles for breakfast. Most of all, she needed a bath. In the corridor to the living room, where she was hoping to find Bidias, Damienne ran into a native woman emerging from a bedroom. No mistaking the disdain in her eyes. She had beautiful braids, a full mouth, and a clean pagne tied around her chest. Her grimace at the sight of Damienne's dirty clothes would, mere days ago, have caused Damienne great distress, but she had spent enough time with the Pygmy now to not be bothered. The barefoot Negress passed without responding to the white woman's greeting. At the end of the hallway, she turned left and disappeared.

People were gathered in the living room. In her current state, Damienne didn't see how she could be properly introduced. A door behind her opened and the redhead from the night before came out of the same bedroom as the Negress. He greeted Damienne politely and went into the living room.

Bidias was at the far end of the room, and Damienne waited for him to come to her. Bidias told her he might, at best, manage half a bucket of water for her to bathe and rinse her clothes, but there was no soap. Things would improve once it rained. Damienne followed him to a medium-sized room that had been repurposed as a kitchen for the circumstances. Three stones had been placed in the middle of the floor to hold up a pot, beneath which a wood fire had been lit. There was no other equipment. Four natives were peeling manioc and chatting, and her guide chatted with them. The girl who had stared so disdainfully at Damienne in the hallway was among them. She'd been laughing loudly but froze at the sight of the white woman. Damienne understood that this Negress considered her a rival. Without waiting for the other to declare war (as the Yambassa woman had, by spitting on the ground), she spoke to Bidias.

"Bidias, how many women are there in the house?"

"Counting you, there are two, madame."

"And what is the name of the other?"

"Sikini, madame."

"Tell Sikini I am not here to take her man. And warn her that, while I'm not looking for a fight, I will answer blow for blow if it comes to it. Can you tell her that in Bafia?"

"Yes, madame."

"Bidias, please also tell her that I would be pleased to wear one of her beautiful pagnes, if she has another in her room."

❧

A long moment of silence followed Damienne's appearance in the living room where people had gathered, but not to chat. Days of doing without meant personal hygiene wasn't anyone's top concern, but what dominated the room was not so much the smell but the general discouragement. Despair—whether from fear of dying or of dying *in Africa*—was evident in the men's faces and their scruffy beards. Fifteen pairs of silent eyes stayed glued to Damienne, who was dressed according to the local standards of feminine elegance. Sikini had tied the pagne herself, after they'd made peace, and taken away Damienne's dress and boots to wash.

Then pandemonium broke loose outside, and everyone rushed to the windows. Even Damienne went to peek through the slits. At the back of the enormous courtyard, natives wearing shorts fashioned from animal skins were waving their arms around the smoldering remains of the bonfires. Someone declared there were only half as many as the day before, but Damienne still thought there were a lot of them. It was depressing. She leaned against a wall. A night's sleep with the luxury of a pillow had done her good, and the half bucket of cold water had helped clear her mind. Damienne reviewed her situation and concluded again that worrying about a girl like Edoa was foolish; it had already cost her dearly and now it was high time she focus on her own problems. One little thought she'd worked to suppress since she'd awoken was suddenly foremost in her mind: if this continued another five days, the situation would turn to their advantage. No one but Damienne knew that Chief Atangana had given Dr. Jamot another three days, add two days to reach Bafia on foot . . . So, she calculated, five days before the king of the Ewondos would arrive in Bafia and demand the rioters tell him where his niece was. Based on what Damienne had seen, there would be a lot of commotion and, while the natives were busy fighting among themselves, the whites could take advantage of the situation to slip out and alert the authorities in Yaoundé. While this might seem cynical, it also seemed sensible to Damienne. She scanned the room for Administrator Cournarie, but he wasn't there. She promised herself she'd fill him in as soon as he appeared. All she really needed to know was if the food and water would last; they just needed to make it through a week of siege and they'd be saved. Knowing that, Damienne already felt much less somber when the inevitable ritual of introductions began, once everyone had finally turned away from the windows.

They looked like zombies. Damienne brazenly confirmed that she had come to replace Dr. Monier, convinced her imposture would hold at least until the end of the siege. She realized almost everyone in the region's colonial administration had taken refuge under their chief officer's roof. Cournarie still hadn't returned, so the redhead took charge of the formalities. He introduced himself as head of "the special agency," meaning he was the treasurer and tax collector. Then he introduced Damienne to the chief of the post office and to the chief of the school district. That brave soul bemoaned, between nostalgic memories, the seven pupils who didn't return after their first recess. She also met the manager of the commissary. But it was Pouget, the chief of the brigade of gendarmes, that most interested Damienne; a handsome thirty-year-old, the kind of man you don't expect to see in a police uniform, especially not in a savage colony. But when he introduced his two colleagues, Damienne ceased wondering how they'd been overrun by natives armed with fetishes; in a real country, no one would've even let those two guard a lighthouse. Their chief spoke of his vigorous efforts to combat the law of the jungle which, transmitted through generations over millennia, natives accepted without question, and admitted that he found it more rewarding to stand in for Administrator Cournarie in the customary court, presiding over plenary sessions and recognizing those who wanted to speak.

Damienne turned her attention to Le Toullec, Dr. Monier's assistant, who introduced four health auxiliaries and two native nurses, one

of whom still wore his uniform, a white helmet and khaki shorts. Le
Toullec told her there were seven other members of the medical team in
the house—they were organized into shifts for keeping watch and sleeping. Trying to look official, Damienne gravely nodded her approval.
He went on to explain that, of all their equipment, only the medical
kits that had been on site at the start of the revolt had been saved. That
meant there were only eight kits, not counting the one Thouvenin had
taken. Le Toullec regretted the loss of the most fully stocked, the kit
agent Bertignac and nurse Edoa had had the day they'd been attacked
in Donenkeng. Seeing Damienne jump, Le Toullec reassured her that
the kit would eventually be recovered, his two colleagues were probably
still on the run, given the circumstances, and . . . Damienne lost track
of what he was saying. They had to call her name before she took the
ear of corn Sikini held out to her. A *boy* followed the native woman,
carrying a pan filled with pieces of steaming manioc. Cournarie finally
appeared. He spoke first to the chief of the gendarmes. Damienne pretended not to notice. A quick head count told her there was a total of
fourteen people there who'd been part of the medical team before things
had fallen apart. They were all of interest, and she was eager to strike up
a conversation with each of them, because they knew Edoa. Her next
priority was to figure out who knew most about her. She had one day
left to find her. If she didn't achieve her mission by then, she still had
her backup plan. Nibbling her corn, Damienne glanced at the native
nurses, who just kept smiling, as if everything were fine.

Before Damienne could do anything, Administrator Cournarie
started making eyes at her. Although he'd been in Africa for years, it
seemed he'd only just discovered there might be something tempting
wrapped up in a bit of pagne. Damienne listened as he praised her courage, working hard not to show her irritation at his outrageous sexism
wrapped in platitudes. While her host prattled on, she kept tabs on the
two native nurses. After apologizing for not having welcomed her more

appropriately, Cournarie urged Monier's fake replacement to be patient, promising that things would change in the next day or so.

"How can you be sure?" Damienne asked.

"Because today I go to Donenkeng for the coronation ceremony," he replied. "Can you imagine, the leader of these crazy fools, Abouem, the man who did the unthinkable, is going to be named chief of his village, and I have to preside over the ceremony!"

"You can't, it would be suicide!"

"Not going would be more than just a dereliction of duty. This subdivision is vast: seventeen villages divided among three clans, each led by a mostly legitimate chief, but that's not the issue. At this ceremony, twenty leaders of different levels will gather a few kilometers from here. They're bound by a collection of primitive rituals, mystical to say the least, and they will orchestrate the investiture. I only come in at the end to confer legitimacy to the whole proceeding.

"Among those august individuals, eight owe their title to me outright. If I put my papers together, I could change their lives, reveal things the people will never otherwise know, but I won't, provided these majesties behave reasonably toward us. Believe me, I have stories about the chiefs under my power—they can refuse me nothing. Even the elder leader of the coterie, with his long white beard and finely carved wood pipe. With just half his wives, we could repopulate Courtecon or Bezonvaux in a matter of three years; and you know Africans respect nothing more than age and virility. He will listen to me and, in turn, he will be listened to. But, to be safe—because the people do have a legitimate reason to be angry—I'll offer something to the other chiefs too. I'll promise protection and medals, which they'll receive in Yaoundé from the French high commissioner himself. I'm sure to win another five to my cause, and on the morning after his coronation, calmer heads will prevail and put Abouem in his place.

"This morning, at cockcrow, I sent a *boy* with the message that I intend to participate in the ceremony; I just received the elder's reply a few minutes ago. The assembly of chiefs accepted my petition and will grant me safe passage for twenty-four hours for a delegation of three people."

Two polite smiles brought the conversation to a close, and Damienne rushed to the kitchen.

Sikini was polishing the white woman's boots, reusing the water used to wash first the manioc and then her clothes. The other *boys* were sitting together on a long bench of roughly hewn wood. The Pygmy guide, sitting on the floor in a corner, was sharpening a stick. Everyone was listening, more or less, to the nurse still wearing his white pith helmet, who seemed to think his costume gave him the right to reprimand other natives. The second nurse, closer to the door, roused himself at the sight of the white woman; he held out his clasped hands, hoping to be helpful. She reached out to shake his hand and asked him to remind her of his name. The others, now aware of the white woman's presence, plastered servile smiles on their faces—all except the Pygmy, that is.

"Madame, my name is Priso David," replied the nurse, whose hand Damienne still held.

"And mine is Abanda Thadée, madame," said the helmeted nurse, inserting himself in the conversation.

"So, gentlemen, who can tell me about Edoa?" Damienne asked.

"I can, madame!" they said at once.

They glared at each other to decide who would speak first, and Damienne had to intervene to prevent an argument. Sikini set the boots down by the window, having done her best, and left. Priso, invited to speak first, smirked at his friend and said that Edoa was a worthy woman, so good at giving injections she'd been authorized to give shots to men as well as women. He noted with regret that though he, Priso, was just as adept, he still hadn't been authorized to give shots to women. He added that Edoa was exceptional because she knew how to cook couscous three ways, sewed her own aprons and dresses, could braid her own hair, and could even shave a man's head using a shard of glass. He hadn't ever seen her catch a catfish, but he bet she knew how. He recognized that she had two flaws: she spoke to men any way she pleased, and worse, she'd dared to eat some viper on a feast day in her uncle's palace—publicly flouting a dietary taboo for women. Given that, he understood why no one yet had asked for her hand.

Sikini returned, removed the lid from a pot on the fire with her bare hand, grimacing at the escaping steam, tested a piece of manioc floating in the boiling water with her finger, then put the lid back on the pot, added more fuel to the fire, said a few things in Bafia, and left the room again. The Pygmy had started to skewer two beetles when Abanda, the helmeted nurse, cleared his throat and began speaking.

He'd known Edoa for years, since he was the son of an important dignitary in her uncle's court. They were, in fact, cousins, and to prove it he recited two genealogies to the sixth generation, by which point he still hadn't identified a common ancestor. Damienne had to insist that she believed him to keep him from going back any further. He tried to revisit the incident about her eating viper; he himself had witnessed the anger of the notables, but Damienne managed to get him back to the point. Angry at being interrupted each time he tried to explain something important, Abanda passed over some ten years of essential details. When he finally got to their shared time at the Instructional Center in Ayos, Damienne paid close attention. They'd apparently had to hold great palavers with all the local chiefs before Edoa was allowed to participate in the mobile testing units. Afraid of discouraging him entirely, Damienne forced herself to listen to a half dozen anecdotes before Abanda finally came to more recent events. Claiming he'd been sent to Bafia expressly to watch over his cousin, he alleged Edoa had a habit of disappearing during the medical tours. Once, she'd even disappeared for three whole days—but eventually she returned. He confirmed she was a good nurse, intelligent and resourceful, even if sometimes impertinent. He almost stopped there, but then he remembered, the night before her last tour, his cousin had seemed unwell and had even gone behind the health center to vomit. Abanda was struck by that because he'd never seen her sick before. He turned to his colleague Priso as his witness, and Priso confirmed he'd confided as much to him. Abanda thought since the Bafias hadn't exhibited his cousin, dead or alive, she had cut through the bush and was on her way to Yaoundé. He concluded by asserting that Edoa would certainly reach her destination, provided she'd managed to ditch agent Bertignac.

With the flourish of a master chef, Ndongo examined his beetle kebab and put it back on the embers. Before thanking the two nurses, Damienne asked if Edoa had any close friends or confidants on the medical team. They said Edoa was on friendly terms with everyone, including the Pygmy porters. They conferred for a moment before adding that she spent hours talking with Madame Monier, who appreciated her company and even loaned her books, which Edoa took on her tours.

The conversation with Priso and Abanda hadn't produced the results Damienne hoped for. They'd only confirmed that she'd been there when the revolt broke out. Edoa was part of the unit led by Bertignac, whom the villagers at Donenkeng had turned against. Damienne recalled what the deserter Thouvenin had said when he'd explained the source of the conflict. Thouvenin had gone on at length about Bertignac, but hadn't made any mention of Edoa. He'd spoken highly of her when Damienne asked, without mentioning she'd been there during the first attack, perhaps even fallen victim to it! That didn't seem like a meaningless oversight to her. Hoping to dig into the question further, she changed her mind and decided to keep her cards close to her chest when talking with Cournarie.

If she told anyone the real reason she was there, that would put an end to her secret mission. She didn't want to give up on finding Edoa and saving the day unless she was sure she had no chance of success. And that meant she still needed to learn all she could about Edoa. In that light, talking with the nurses Priso and Abanda hadn't actually been a waste of time: they'd fleshed out the portrait of this young native woman, full of personality, quite competent, and well educated to boot. And just maybe Damienne would be able to meet her herself before it was too late. So Damienne decided to return to the living room where everyone else was gathered.

Rounding the corner in the hallway, Damienne almost ran right into Sikini coming from the opposite direction. She was carrying the remains of the corn people had eaten, and Damienne found the odor both appealing and unsettling; it reminded her of the couscous she'd been offered in the hut of the favorite of the Yambassa chief. Sikini smiled by way of apology. Damienne thought that a man like the red-head, a treasurer–tax collector deep in the bush without much else to see, had good reason to succumb to the charms of this native woman. Instead of moving on, Sikini said something that sounded to Damienne like a riddle. "What?" she exclaimed, and the Negress repeated the phrase, again ending with a familiar sounding word. Suspecting this was a clue, Damienne motioned for Sikini to follow her to the kitchen, where she had been headed anyway. The *boys*, the nurses, and the Pygmy were still there, although there was one less beetle on the skewer. After leading Sikini to Abanda, Damienne again said "What?" and the young woman repeated her riddle.

"What is she saying?"

"She says she knows where Edoa is now, madame."

"Tell her to go on!"

Sikini spoke and the translation followed:

"She says Edoa is staying in a hut in the chief's compound in Donenkeng; she only comes out to bathe. Her meals are brought by a co-wife of Abouem's deceased mother, who was his wet nurse. Her clothes are washed and dried in the courtyard, including her *dokita* uniform. Everyone in Donenkeng knows she's there. Sikini learned this from a cousin who is from Donenkeng."

After this, Damienne had only one goal in mind: convince Administrator Cournarie to make her part of the delegation going to

Donenkeng for Abouem's investiture. There was no easy way to suggest this. Not fifteen minutes before, Damienne had been dissuading him from going, and now she needed him to take her along. On top of that, the delegation was limited to three people—and two of those spots were clearly reserved for the head of the subdivision and the head of the gendarmerie. That left one spot, if by some miracle it hadn't already been given to someone else.

Cournarie listened to her politely. Then he began by praising her bravery, as she'd expected, but reminded her that the natives were unpredictable and she was a doctor, a woman, and white, in a particularly hostile environment. In response, Damienne stressed that she was also a medical officer, second class, soon to be promoted, and most of all, she wanted to see firsthand the attitudes of those she was supposed to treat. Assuming, of course, as she did, that the diplomatic maneuver the administrator had outlined would produce the desired results in the assembly of traditional chiefs. Flattered, Cournarie agreed to consider the question. But since he'd already let two people know they'd be going, he couldn't promise.

After their conversation, Le Toullec introduced the other members of the medical team to Damienne, both whites and Blacks. Instead of providing her with additional information about Edoa, as she'd hoped, he went on about Bertignac. She let him talk, since she needed to kill time while waiting for a signal from Cournarie.

"François Bertignac"—Le Toullec told her—"arrived in Cameroon in 1925. He was assigned to the Bafia subdivision, and worked here for the past four years. In charge of the villages of Bigna and Kiki. Hardworking. A nice guy. He adapted quickly to the environment, and even asked permission to reside in Bigna, where even still some natives like him, despite everything. He integrated into the communal life of his adopted village, and even learned some of the local language. He contracted sleeping sickness, was treated by Dr. Monier, and recovered. During his convalescence at the health center, he caused a stir by cooking corn couscous with manioc leaves, the local speciality. As soon as he was cured, he asked to return to work and went back to live in the same village. He was known, too, for the guitar he carried everywhere; he played pretty well, whenever there was downtime. Before taking responsibility for Donenkeng, due to Dr. Monier's absence, Bertignac had no noticeable troubles anywhere. He had only made friends. Everyone thinks that, given all he's learned from his contact with the natives, he'll be able to survive in the forest—unless he's hidden in the hut of an admirer in Bigna."

The chanting had started up again outside, making the mood inside darker. Through the window, Damienne saw natives covered in white powder, dancing, waving batons and spears. Their dance held a certain elegance, although, despite the joy visible on their faces, you could tell they weren't just playing around, even with the women's bare breasts and lasciviously shaking hips and the men's shining pectorals.

She remembered she needed to speak with her guide, to let him know she intended to go to Donenkeng, and she hoped he would accompany her. But again, everything depended on Cournarie's response.

People had gathered at the other end of the living room. The red-head, Provat, was holding forth. Damienne started toward the kitchen when he, with a discreet wave, invited her to join his audience, composed of the two gendarmes, a health auxiliary, and one other man. They had three rifles and were planning to break through the siege if Cournarie's maneuver failed. They'd start at noon the following day. They clearly didn't share the administrator's optimism because they spoke as if his strategy was already doomed. If the colonial delegation was taken hostage, they had a plan—which consisted of shooting their way out and escaping along the Mbam River. Once their plan was finalized, the group dispersed.

Damienne sat for a moment and gathered her thoughts. Cournarie and the chief of the gendarmerie were speaking by a window; they were finalizing the delegation and the role it would play in the coming hours. If they had noticed the group gathered around Provat, they were unaware of the reason why. Damienne thought they would be the last to realize what was being planned right under their noses. Based on her observations of the plotters, she didn't imagine allying herself with them, but she was careful not to reveal her disapproval in case she might need to take them up on their offer. None of them seemed likely to survive two days in the forest, even with the assistance of a Pygmy. They were tenderfoots who'd found themselves a small corner of the bush where, despite their evident mediocrity, they seemed to think they were saints; Provat, with the pinched face of a religious zealot and his dainty little hands, didn't look like someone ready to fetch his own bath water. No, he was more likely the kind who wouldn't think twice about taking advantage of the natives' complacency to have himself carried from village to village on a sedan chair. Damienne was just wondering who had decided to send such a character to collect taxes in Africa when there was a clear need for used car salesmen back in France when Cournarie gestured for her to join them.

She was told that she would be part of the delegation attending the coronation of His Majesty Abouem II, chief for life of Donenkeng and, by virtue of that position, fee assessor at the customary court in Bafia. The only condition imposed upon Damienne was that she wear her boots, whether they were dry or not, because appearances mattered, even in an unknown corner of the bush.

Two notables had been assigned to escort the administrative delegation to Donenkeng. They appeared on the veranda wearing off-white pagnes tied around their waists, foreheads and forearms shiny with palm oil, toes exposed to the air. They were supposed to arrive at ten o'clock, and so finally appeared at 12:27. As they walked with the three whites through groups of dancers wearing hieratic masks, the two notables showed little interest in making up for lost time. They stopped for long exchanges with the insurgents, and even though she hadn't exactly mastered Bafia, Damienne understood they were telling them not to let anyone else leave the house. Then the group went toward the village center. Women with large wood or aluminum earrings stood in front of their identical huts (it was a miracle some hadn't already collapsed) and stared as the group passed, while their dirty children munched on some unrecognizable fruit with orange flesh and a spiky pit. The few men remaining there sat on wooden benches in front of their huts, canes by their feet, blinking rapidly. The same smell that had struck Damienne the night before rose up: it came from hundreds of fruits lying on both sides of the path, fermenting in the grass—clearly, the natives didn't even notice. Damienne wished her interpreter were there—he'd have told her the name of the exotic fruit—but she knew her guide was far more useful. Just before they'd left, he'd spoken to her in his whispery voice; Damienne hoped that meant he was following her. But he was nowhere to be seen.

At the foot of the hill, there was a fork in the path, and they turned right. For the first time, Damienne saw what remained of the Bafia Health Center: one smoldering corner post. The flames had charred half of a nearby avocado tree. They'd been lucky: the rainy season was lingering and the grass was still wet, so the fire hadn't spread. Everyone was silent as the group passed that sinister scene and plunged into the forest.

There were fewer huts, and fewer fruit trees too. For half an hour, the only sounds were their footsteps, the rustling of ferns as they passed, and occasionally, the loud chirping of a flock of sparrows. One notable led the way, holding carefully to the edge of his ceremonial pagne, only worn for investitures. Cournarie followed, with Damienne close behind. After her came the gendarme—who, without his rifle, no longer looked the part—and then the other notable. There was nothing particularly reassuring about walking toward Donenkeng, yet Damienne felt calmer than she had in previous days. Maybe because she wasn't the only white person, the sole focus of hate-filled stares.

Eventually among the trees to her left, she spotted smoke. Then they heard the clamor of a village, sounds growing clearer as they approached. One hut, then another. A compound, children, women, a man leaning against a mango tree, who turned his head to listen as they approached, and stared with blank, sightless eyes. Their gait seemed almost confident as they came into Donenkeng.

✿

Donenkeng was a large village. In the center of the spacious court-yard, Damienne saw the shelter covered with now partially dried palm fronds where tables set up for the last medical unit still stood, strewn with the equipment they'd abandoned. Nothing had been touched. The huts were in a row, no space between them and woven mats covering the doors and windows. Only the chief's residence stood out from the other compounds—there was an enormous hut at the front, attempting to look majestic with its tall conical straw-covered roof. Beside and somewhat behind it were a crowd of huts like the others—maybe that's where the many widows of the recently deceased chief lived. Most of them would be taken on by the new chief, as custom dictated. A walkway lined with woven palm fronds marked the entrance to the compound. In the chief's courtyard, several shelters were occupied by delegations of notables from nearby villages. Damienne's eyes were lingering on one shelter when suddenly she saw a headdress of leaves and feathers. She nearly jumped out of her skin. How could she forget the witch doctor? Teketekete, with his flyswatter under one arm, was prancing among other, more amiable faces. Damienne averted her eyes, but the witch doctor had spotted her: she was the only blond in all of the region's chiefdoms. Still, Damienne clung to a shred of hope that the witch doctor wouldn't recognize her without her nun's habit. She reflexively touched her waist and realized she wasn't wearing the belt of amulets the Pygmy had made for her. She'd taken it off that morning before washing—she must have left it in the administrator's residence. A European woman of science, a doctor, Damienne didn't believe in fetishes, other than those the priest brandished in church every Sunday. She believed in herself and in logic.

There were crowds of people. Damienne kept asking and re-asking herself the same question: Could she do anything without being noticed? Everyone there was well dressed. The men had donned boubous and chechias, the women were draped in beautiful pagnes. Of course, almost everyone was barefoot, but the seemingly unavoidable backdrop of dirty children was nowhere to be found. Those that hadn't been locked up were wandering around with bare bottoms, but at least they were clean. And the young women! They were everywhere, some with neat braids and colorful strings woven through their locks, others with a crest of hair, others still with shaved heads. They were all displaying their opulent breasts. Damienne caught Cournarie ogling, but the gendarme kept his eyes to himself.

They all seemed to be enjoying themselves, but immediately stopped smiling when Damienne managed to catch their eye. The hostility was plain. But if she hoped to find Edoa and speak with her, she'd need an ally. In the meantime, her first goal was to identify possible escape routes. Now that they were in the heart of Bafia, surrounded by vengeful natives, Cournarie's strategy seemed so uncertain, and she almost regretted not having suggested staying put and waiting for help to arrive.

Next to the shelters filled with dignitaries, in front of the palm-lined walkway leading to the main house, stood the traditional chiefs of the subdivision. Even knowing they were just puppets of the colonial administration, it was impressive to see them gathered in their finery. Some wore boubous, others had layers of necklaces adorning their bare chests, all held scepters. A sneer was plastered on each of His Majesties' faces. Cournarie reassured the members of his delegation by showing off his mastery of African etiquette. Without removing his colonial helmet, with a grimace that would have been funny if it weren't for the chance of the whole country going up in flames, he embraced the old man at the head of the line. The other two had to follow suit, and the greetings went on for a good twenty minutes. Damienne was embraced by all the chiefs. Some groped her breasts. The Yambassa chief devoured her with his eyes, making it clear to Damienne that she had been recognized; she was relieved to realize he couldn't give orders in someone else's village. But getting back to Yaoundé—if the outcome of the festivities didn't render it impossible—was going to be complicated, unless Damienne found another path through the forest, or a gun. Among the chiefs was one blind man, who had clearly been dragged there so he could fulfill his traditional duties. Murmurs ran through the crowd when the white men embraced him, and Damienne noticed several natives spit on the ground. They still had to embrace Chief Abouem.

Abouem stood at the entrance to his compound, the very image of calm. He couldn't have been even thirty-five. He didn't have the bulging muscles of the young men standing behind him like so many guard dogs, but he had a natural elegance. He was wearing a simple, unadorned pagne slung over one shoulder and zebu-leather sandals. Despite his eyes—which betrayed evident exhaustion—he had a charm that Damienne hadn't expected to find in the heart of the forest. Chief Abouem's smirk wasn't as crass as the others'. Even his kinky hair didn't detract from his charms. Damienne was ready to embrace him whether protocol called for it or not, but Cournarie whispered that no one was to touch Abouem until he'd received the symbols of his power.

A chorus of shouts brought her quickly back to attention; Abouem walked forward, his hands outstretched. Damienne watched everyone bow down before one man, and that increased her anxiety. The women pressed their foreheads to the ground, then rose as one, ululating loudly; the adult men moved closer to their leader, holding out clasped hands in a sign of allegiance, and then backed away. The young men were in a frenzy, they seemed to have lost their minds. This scene from another time unsettled the young woman. The simplicity with which Africans put their faith in their chief was both admirable and rare—and it suited everyone there, including people like Cournarie.

Damienne felt a little sad knowing this handsome chief, so obviously adored, wouldn't have the idyllic reign he deserved because of the democratic conspiracy afoot in the council that even now greeted his triumphant entrance. But the public phase of his investiture was about to begin. The people were only allowed to witness the folkloric part of the ceremony, the shamanistic rituals having taken place the night before, shielded from the eyes of the uninitiated.

All the chiefs, including the blind one, circled Abouem and the elder chief, whose white beard and hair were the visible signs of his integrity. He was smoking a pipe and held in his hands an ornate baton, different from the others. Suddenly Abouem rushed to him and, grabbing the baton from the elder's hands, brandished it like a trophy. Cheers and ululations exploded all over the courtyard; bare-chested girls performed a dance Damienne deemed even more elegant than the one outside Administrator Cournarie's house. The venerable elder placed a chechia on Abouem's head, then erupted with impassioned words of praise while holding the hand of the newly crowned chief aloft. Everyone bowed again. One by one the chiefs approached Abouem, spoke briefly, shook his hand, then touched his forehead. As they pledged their support to Abouem, Damienne stared, trying to decipher who would challenge him. She couldn't identify anyone in particular—they all seemed like serious people. After the ceremony, the colonial administrator was allowed to say a few words, which no one translated and so remained a mystery for nine out of ten villagers. The essential thing was that he speak, not that he be understood. Only then did Damienne, following Cournarie and Pouget, enjoy the privilege of embracing a traditional African chief of her own volition. That brought the official ceremonies to an end, and the festivities began.

While the people celebrated their new chief, the whites were ushered into the main house of the chief's compound, where a wicker table and stools were waiting for them. As soon as they sat, steaming plates of vegetables and corn couscous were served, and Damienne finally got to taste the dish that had made her mouth water in Yambassa. She dug into it, after rinsing her hand in a bowl of water. Cournarie made a show of seeming to eat, but then went to the shelter where the chiefs sat with the white-bearded elder.

The people had already danced so much and the festivities were just getting started. Damienne decided to walk around the shelters to gauge the amount of freedom their hosts intended to give them. In the courtyard, groups of women continued to dance to the rhythm of a drum and a tom-tom played by two musicians drunk on raffia wine. The ambiance was celebratory. It was hard to believe these were the same people who, after losing their previous chief and his named successor, had started a rebellion and set fire to the health center, all while apparently holding a nurse prisoner. The people seemed less on edge, although occasional glares reminded Damienne that she wasn't walking around the displays at a colonial exposition. After a moment's hesitation, she decided to wander off to the right, away from the shelter where the chiefs were gathered. Outside, wood had been stacked, ready to be lit when the time came—clearly, this was going to be a long night.

Empty bowls disappeared into a hut across the path and opposite the chief's compound, from which they emerged filled with food again. There were dishes of game, fish, and other food wrapped in leaves. People ate in small groups, happy to eat together. Women took care of the service.

Damienne noticed a girl stuffing herself with couscous while nursing a baby. It was actually the baby who caught Damienne's attention; something was off about its color. She moved as close as she dared to get a better look: the baby was mixed race. She supposed it was possible some of the more open-minded health auxiliaries from the medical units had left something other than medicines, and blindness, behind in the villages. It wasn't the first time Damienne had seen a mixed child in Cameroon. In Ayos, at the Instructional Center where she'd spent her first two weeks, she'd crossed paths several times with a young woman going toward the nearby river with a pretty little girl, almost white, two or three years old, strapped to her back.

Making her way around the side of the main house, Damienne almost collided with a young woman who towered over her and stared with expressionless eyes. She had a cleanly shaved head, a perfectly flat belly, and a mango pit dangling around her neck. Damienne thought her troubles were about to begin again. To avoid a confrontation, she kept her eyes locked on her breasts—they were insolently perky.

With a hand still covered in the remains of her last mouthful of couscous, the girl grabbed hold of the white woman's hair and pulled. Damienne cried out. Convinced the gleaming locks were in fact the stranger's own hair, her face lit up. For a minute she admired the blond tresses. Unfortunately, the chief had ordered that no one lay a hand on the white people before daybreak. But she was patient. At dawn, she'd have her eyes on the white woman; if she fell, no one else would get their hands on her head. She planned to attach the beautiful locks to her own head, making her the resident white woman. She caressed the gleaming hair again and went on her way.

As Damienne gathered her wits, she noticed an older woman going around the side of the main house with a bowl of food and decided to follow her. The woman turned right and then disappeared. Damienne almost ran after her, but thought it best to keep walking. Before she could turn the corner and see where the woman had gone, two big men appeared, blocking her way. Just the looks on their faces made her back up, and they followed to make sure she returned to the other guests.

Before going back to the living room, Damienne spotted her Pygmy guide. She was no longer surprised by his serenity; with all that couscous circulating, the shameless women, and his belt of amulets, he had everything he needed. As for Cournarie, he was deep in discussions with three dignitaries, while the elder spoke to Abouem and poked him with his pipe. Pouget hadn't moved; he just kept showing his lack of diplomatic savvy in the living room, where the gourd of raffia wine he'd been served sat untouched. He relaxed a bit seeing Damienne return. Without even a glance in his direction, she went toward the door at the back of the room, which had to lead to the bedrooms or the rear of the chief's compound, where the small huts she'd glimpsed earlier stood. No one had come from that direction. Aware that she was crossing a line, Damienne headed into the belly of the chief's compound. She knew if she got caught, it would be the end not only of her, but also of all the whites left in the Bafia subdivision.

Damienne hurried through a dark hallway that smelled of wet earth. The thatched roof was high enough—there was no ceiling, per se—and the rays of light filtering through the cracks helped her to see her way. Holding her breath, Damienne tiptoed through two chambers, their windows blocked by woven screens. A second hallway led her off toward the right, and a third brought her back to the left. There was light at the end: a door that opened onto the huts in the back. Before venturing out, she carefully looked around—no one in sight.

There were three huts. From the first she heard women's voices, some sobbing and others comforting. Damienne moved quickly past that hut. Not a sound came from the other two. She barely touched the screen over the second one's door when it tumbled to the ground— happily without making a sound. But Damienne's heart started to calm down only when she realized there was no one inside. In too much of a hurry to replace the screen, she ran toward the last hut. She reached out to push the screen aside, then hesitated, and decided instead to knock. A second of silence, then two, three . . . She was just about to retreat to the living room when the screen was gently pulled aside and a young woman appeared. As soon as she saw her, Damienne knew who she was.

III: The Obsessed

"Are you Edoa, the nurse?"

"Yes, I'm Edoa."

"My name is Damienne Bourdin. I've been looking for you. Follow me."

"Follow you where?"

"Come now! We have to act quickly if we want any chance of making it out of the village."

"I have no intention of leaving the village. And you shouldn't be here. Go!"

"Listen, I've come from Yaoundé. You can trust me. Dr. Jamot sent me. He gave me orders to come and save you and—"

"Save me from what? Who told Dr. Jamot I was in danger?"

"Um . . ."

"You need to get out of here immediately. If you don't, there's nothing I can do for you!"

"Edoa, I am ord—"

Damienne was cut off midsentence. Edoa grabbed her arm and pulled her inside the hut. She pushed her behind the screen and, with one finger on her lips, whispered, "Shh!" Outside, a woman was calling the nurse; Edoa quickly went outside. Right where Damienne had stood moments before, the two women calmly chatted in Bafia. Inside the hut, Damienne leaned against the earthen wall. Edoa had just saved her life! So many questions swirled in her mind, and all her fears came flooding back. She needed to pull herself together. She focused on her surroundings. There was a pole suspended between two walls, just above head level, on which clothes were hung. Below that, a bamboo bed frame, a thick mattress of dried grass, partially covered with pagnes, and a pile of clean laundry on top; the only window was blocked; on the ground, a bowl with a little bit of leftover couscous; on the left, a medical case. The screen moved again and Damienne held her breath. It was Edoa and she was alone.

"You, you can't stay here," the nurse whispered. "That woman will be back soon to give me a hot-water massage, and she'll come inside. You have to go back to the others. I'll see if the path is clear. Don't move, I'll be right back."

"But I—"

"Shh!"

Edoa went out, pulling the screen closed behind her. She wasn't acting the way Damienne had expected, and that really unsettled her. Nothing made sense. She'd spent much of the past days trying to imagine this African woman who learned to read and write and then became a nurse. She had sketched a hundred portraits of this native woman in her mind. But the young woman she'd just met bore no resemblance to any of those clichés. Damienne realized she might not have the upper hand after all; it made her feel furious. She could hear women crying in the hut next door and the soft voices of those helping them, muffled by the sound of the tom-tom. On the bed, something seemed to move, but Damienne didn't have a chance to look closely, because the screen slid open and Edoa came back in.

"The path is clear, now hurry—"

"But I have to talk to you!"

"Not now. Go to the left—"

"Edoa, Edoa, listen to me! What I have to say is important, a matter of life and death."

"Not here. Behind these huts there's a path down toward the *marigot*, the stream. I'll be there in twenty or thirty minutes. If you want to talk, meet me there. But don't let anyone see you. Now go back to the main house, follow the hallway and stay with Messieurs Cournarie and Pouget. They're alone in the living room. Hurry."

Edoa had already pulled the screen closed. Alone outside, Damienne had to do as she was told. She retraced her steps and, after zigzagging through the hallways of the chief's house, made it back to the living room where the administrator and the gendarme were deep in conversation.

Before either of them could ask her anything, Damienne explained she'd had to take care of an urgent need under a stand of banana trees behind the huts. She couldn't tell them the whole truth, or waste time trying to mollify them, but she knew she'd need their help, especially Cournarie's. Now that she had found Edoa, she had to bring her back to her uncle, the great Chief Atangana, to prevent him from sending a war party to punish the Bafias. And she had to do this before the day after next.

But to even make it back to Yaoundé from Bafia in two days would be nothing short of a miracle, even if there were no issues getting through all those villages filled with blind people and rebels. If there was any chance of success, they had to be on their way before sunrise—and given Edoa's surprising attitude, that seemed very unlikely.

Damienne wanted to help Dr. Jamot, but she couldn't reduce the threat to security in Bafia to getting just one young nurse out, even if she was a princess. There were all the others, white and Black, left in Cournarie's residence, people she'd eaten corn and manioc with, people with whom she'd trembled at the chants and shouts of a delirious horde of sweaty madmen. She couldn't ignore the fates of people she knew. Most were her compatriots or colleagues, each with their own story, their own obsessions. Whether by choice or by circumstances beyond their control, they had ended up there, just as she had. And Africa was their last chance at redemption. In some of their eyes she'd seen the flash of a thirst for revenge, of their burning desire, fueled by adversity, for a triumphant return. Whether she managed to get Edoa out or not would make no difference for them. They were in danger, and maintaining the status quo until Chief Atangana arrived to punish their assailants wouldn't necessarily improve their chances. The offensive planned by Provat and his gang was even riskier, far more likely to result in a full-out race war. If nothing stopped the redhead and his accomplices, Damienne worried she'd have even less time to act. Rather than a confrontation between natives of different tribes in five days, there'd be a battle between whites and Blacks in twenty-four hours. It would be impossible to go anywhere in the subdivision, or even beyond its borders, and Damienne would have to hole up in the forest, if she even made it out alive. That thought made her look at Cournarie in a new light.

But the most pressing thing was to meet Edoa by the *marigot*, behind the huts at the back of the chief's compound. For that, Damienne needed the Pygmy.

The day was almost done. Say what you like, the Bafias know how to dance. Chief Abouem, wearing his chechia and waving his ornate scepter, was dancing wildly among thirteen of his young supporters. They danced in staggered rows, shimmying bare chests and shoulders, one step forward and two steps back—so elegant! Everyone, even the traditional chiefs and guests from all of the clans, looked up from their bowls of couscous to applaud. Around his waist, each dancer wore two belts of finger-length beads knotted with long strands of straw that twirled with every shake of their hips. Some seemed to keep time by waving a flyswatter, their wrists adorned with three ivory bracelets; others shook a shiny little bell whose dizzying clangs added rhythm to the wild beating of the tom-toms. The Pygmy stood between two burly villagers with round cheeks, making him look even smaller in comparison. Noting that he was clapping in time to the music and clearly enjoying it, Damienne promised that, when she had a moment, she'd reconsider her anthropological assessment of the purely primitive nature of Pygmies. As she walked toward her guide, a hand reached out and pulled her back, and she found herself face to face with the chief of the Yambassas.

The Yambassa chief was furious that the white woman had lied to him, because the outfit she was wearing couldn't be worn by a priest's wife. But mostly he was angry she'd escaped before he'd had his way with her. He had intended to keep her for the night, so that everyone would see just who was the most powerful. Thanks to the witch doctor Teketekete's aphrodisiac roots, she would've remembered him for the rest of her days. Maybe she would've even decided to stay with him for good, burnishing his heroic reputation. The chief of the Yambassas was convinced that if people knew he had taken a white woman, it would add to his prestige. By running away, she'd shamed him in the eyes of all the village women, who'd understood full well what he had in mind. What's worse, Boto—the tigress who was his current favorite—had turned him away that evening when he'd gone to her hut. Boto's jealousy was beginning to irritate him, but he'd take care of her later. Now that he'd found the white woman, he was going to make up for lost time. True, she didn't have the posterior of a Yambassa woman, but her chest was okay, and she had a pretty face, if a bit pale. It was good she'd traded in all that cursed black cloth for a respectable outfit: now she looked like a real woman. Since they weren't in his village, where his power was absolute, he couldn't just strip the white woman bare right then and there—although that was what he was dying to do. There were too many chiefs, including envious ones who would like to be in his shoes. While waiting for the right moment to present itself, the chief of the Yambassas intended to keep a close watch on her. He would be vigilant, because the white woman had proven how slippery she was. Worse than a catfish.

Damienne shuddered, then collected herself and tried to project the proud and nonchalant attitude she'd seen in some local women, although that meant running the risk of being treated like one. The distinguished chief, still holding her arm, was in such a state that he frankly seemed capable of anything. Damienne didn't know if the locals made any distinction between a pickup artist and a rapist, since around here a girl was at the mercy of any man who happened upon her alone in a manioc field.

Still, her principal worry was the thought of missing her meeting with Edoa. Suddenly she remembered that the chief of the Yambassas understood French—at least somewhat. So Damienne spoke to him slowly, carefully articulating each word; she convinced him that she'd been looking for him, that the chief administrator was waiting in the living room, hoping to speak with him about serious matters. Before the chief of the Yambassas could sort out what she'd said, she grabbed his hand and dragged him toward the living room, where she promptly left him. A minute later, she had drawn Ndongo away from the spectacle.

❦

Maybe they'd gotten used to seeing her go back and forth across the courtyard. Was that because she was just a woman—even though a white woman? That Damienne was wearing a pagne with bare shoulders had probably made some see her in a more positive light. And she was grateful that the chief of the Yambassas had been seen standing by her side—even if he was a scoundrel, that worked in her favor. This time no one stopped her as she made her way around the chief's compound. And she easily found the path behind the huts that led into the forest.

In the courtyard, she had taken her time speaking to the Pygmy, carefully making all the gestures that went along with her words, as if she were having a regular conversation with anyone else. The time they'd spent together had given her proof of his wisdom, and Damienne knew he'd understand her plans and what she needed, provided he hadn't imbibed too much raffia wine. Still, she was worried. Under the thick canopy of leaves at dusk it was hard to see and each tree could hide a lookout. Damienne was alone in a hostile region, the colonial administrator was unaware of her mission, and she had no support among the traditional chiefs or the local people. She couldn't just blend in—she was the only non-Black woman within a hundred kilometers. One mistake was all it would take and she'd disappear without a trace. She was keenly aware of that.

The path sloped down. She was still mulling over her brief exchange with Edoa behind the screen. If she didn't rise to the occasion when she spoke with Edoa this time, catastrophe would result, and the colony would be engulfed in flames. Damienne passed between the trees, feeling the full weight of the responsibility Dr. Jamot had placed on her slim shoulders.

Once again Ndongo, her irreplaceable guide, saved her. As if by magic he popped out from a bush, took her by the hand, and pulled her behind an enormous termite nest. They had just crouched down when a woman appeared at the end of the trail. Coming from the *marigot*, she passed right by them with an aluminum basin balanced on her head and a bunch of long grass in her hand. It was the same woman Damienne had followed earlier in the chief's courtyard. The same one who had called for Edoa when Damienne was hiding behind the screen. Only one logical conclusion: she had just given Edoa the hot-water massage, leaving the nurse alone by the *marigot*. The Pygmy confirmed this, gesturing to his ward to continue down toward the stream.

Edoa was no longer wearing her loose-fitting dress, she had a pagne tied around her chest like Damienne. Sitting on a boulder, feet dangling in the water, the nurse watched Damienne approach. Edoa appeared more tired than before, her features drawn, almost severe. She wiped her eyes, not wanting Damienne to see she'd been crying. Hot-water massages were definitely not soothing, but she knew how important they were in her situation. She raised her chin, giving the white woman permission to speak.

Damienne took a few seconds to observe the native woman's graceful and expressive face. Before the silence grew unbearable, she said, "I am Dr. Bourdin, now in charge of the Sangmélima subdivision. I came to Bafia on Dr. Jamot's orders to bring you to Yaoundé right away."

Edoa stared at the white woman as if she hadn't said anything at all. So Damienne added, "There will be war if, in two days, you are not back with your uncle, Chief Atangana."

"My place now is with Chief Abouem," Edoa replied.

"You . . ."

"Yes, I am Abouem's fiancée, soon to be his wife. And beyond that, as of a few days ago, I am the mother of his baby."

"Now listen—"

"You don't believe me? Look."

Edoa stood up, undid her pagne and retied it around her waist, freeing full breasts with dusky, hard nipples. She continued to stare at the white woman as she grabbed hold of her breasts. With a light squeeze, two whitish jets squirted out and fell on the calm waters of the *marigot*. A few drops of milk dribbled down her belly as Damienne gasped, eyes bulging out of her head.

"When did you give birth?"

"Four days ago. That's why they're giving me hot-water massages on my belly—they're very painful, but they help you to heal after childbirth."

"But no one told me you were pregnant!"

"No one knew, besides Abouem."

"This is unbelievable!"

"You understand that, given the current situation, I don't want to abandon my fiancé or my baby, despite my admiration and respect for Dr. Jamot and my uncle."

"Edoa, do you realize that because of you, hundreds of lives are in danger, including those of the two people who matter most to you?"

"Dr. Bourdin . . ."

"Yes?"

"You seem nice and I wish you no harm. But have you ever been in love?"

"Um, well . . ."

"Have you even been a mother?"

Damienne froze. How could she answer that question?

"Oh, I see. It wasn't easy?"

"Um, Edoa, I propose we go back to the village, get the baby, and leave. You can always come back later, once your uncle is reassured."

"It's because you're not *African* that you speak of things so naïvely. It's precisely because of this baby that I can't under any circumstances set foot in my village—at least not for a while. For Ewondos, as for most tribes in the country, children born to unwed mothers automatically belong to the mother's parents, whatever her age. Those children that you would call 'bastards' are well received in our clans, cherished even, because of how nature respects the matriarchal line. Since I've been given to no man—there's been no public announcement of my marriage, no exchange of a bride price—I belong entirely to my clan. That's why I didn't attend Abouem's investiture. I've learned there's nothing to be gained by publicly defying taboos.

"Customary law specifies that any children I bear before marriage will always belong to my clan, regardless of what might happen afterward. The baby born here is an Ewondo, and not a Bafia, like his father. If my uncle were to learn of the existence of this child, he'd begin by giving him an Ewondo name, before coming to collect him."

"So, Chief Atangana has two reasons to attack Bafia."

"And I can guarantee that if he'd known about the second, you would not have been sent. My uncle would be here already, especially since the baby is a boy. For better or worse, depending on which side you're on, this baby is the *first grandchild* of the former chief of Donenkeng. The chief had many children from his many wives, but only two sons, and he had the misfortune of dying on the same day as his childless elder son. What it means is that, as I sit talking to you, my baby is the only possible successor to Chief Abouem, who has just been invested. You were at the ceremony. You saw Abouem for yourself. He's the most charismatic and spirited man in the country. Even my uncle, Charles Atangana, who earned diplomas for his studies with the German Pallottine Fathers, who later spoke to Pope Pius X, and then translated the Ewondo language into German, doesn't have his intelligence. Now that Abouem has decided to stand up to the colonists, and because I know both sides, I fear the succession to the chiefdom of Donenkeng will be a matter of contention for a long time. Abouem is aware of this too. That's why, despite our customs and traditions, which we cherish, he won't let his son be taken anywhere. And I stand with him on that."

"Good Lord!"

"I'm sorry for you, but that is how it is."

"How can a girl like you have gotten into such a situation?"

"It's the most natural thing in the world. I can tell you the whole story from the start; we have at least an hour before anyone comes to my hut looking for me. And we won't be disturbed, there's no raffia wine over here.

"My full name is Edoa Débora, and I was born around 1906. My mother was sister to Charles Atangana, paramount chief of the Ewondos and the Benes. Since she was unmarried and died soon after my birth, and since my uncle, the chief, is monogamous, he adopted me as his own. I call him 'papa' because there's no word for 'uncle' in our language. When I was six he enrolled me at the school for the sons of chiefs in Yaoundé. Back then, it wasn't usual for a female person to be anywhere other than the kitchen, the fields, or a bed. I think not having a mother or a father contributed to my luck; since papa was always traveling with the German governor, it was easier to send me to school with my cousins. That was when they were building the great palace for our chief, and even women were needed to help make bricks, so there was no one else to take care of me.

"I'm the first native woman to have learned the German alphabet, and I think still the only one, since we changed to French and girls still rarely go to school. After two years of study, I could read and write. My uncle, the chief, sparked my desire for learning by telling me about his travels in Europe, about the amazing things he'd seen there, the books, and all the important people he'd met—like Emperor Wilhelm II of Germany and King Alfonso XIII of Spain. He promised to take me on his next trip to Germany so I could see locks and keys and mirrors for myself. Alas! Before my uncle could keep his word, war broke out, and he was exiled to Spain. It was five long years before he could return. I still remember the day he came back. They'd planted palm trees all along both sides of the path. Everyone in Yaoundé came to cheer for him, and he was carried triumphantly to his palace. When I saw him, I was so proud, my head spun. During the long years of his absence, I had imagined him crouched in a dank, dark cell, catching roaches to improve his rations. I feared I'd never see him again. And then there he was, fresh as a daisy, wearing a fine suit and tie—nicer than anything we'd ever seen even on the back of a white man. A matching fedora in one hand, a cigar in the other, a nice, neat part near his right temple, and polished two-toned shoes on his feet: he was sublime. The celebration lasted a whole week. For days, between his meetings with groups of notables, I peppered him with questions, and he overwhelmed me with new discoveries. I felt that he was also proud of me, because I had started my studies again from the beginning and now spoke fluent French.

"That same year, 1921, a little before my uncle's return, a white doctor arrived—everyone was talking about him. Rumor had it he was a great witch doctor, unafraid of crossing the forest day or night to take blood from people in faraway villages. They said he had a device that would look at the blood and tell him how many more days a person would live. Some even said he carried a big needle to suck up the good luck of those he was able to stick. In short, he was someone to avoid at all costs. One day I was in the chief's wife's kitchen grinding manioc when a cousin came rushing in, screeching that the evil *dokita* had come to the chief's compound. Curious, I left my mortar and went to the living room. My uncle was chatting with a portly white man with big round cheeks and a thick mustache. As soon as my uncle saw me, he called in French for me to come and shake his visitor's hand, then introduced me to Eugène Jamot. I was fifteen, with some wild ideas and a lot of nerve. I asked Dr. Jamot if he really had a device that let him look at blood; he said yes. I asked him if he stuck people with needles; he said yes. I must have looked suspicious, since he quickly explained why and why it was so important that everyone let themselves get stuck. He confided that he was hoping that my uncle—who had been officially reinstated as paramount chief and who people listened to—would explain this to the people so that good medicine could spread more easily among the villages. I left with a mixed impression, but had no inkling that I had just found my vocation.

"Years went by. Since there were often parties at my uncle's palace, I saw Dr. Jamot several more times. Chief Atangana's support had burnished his reputation in the villages where, through his own hard work, he had won an initial victory over rumor. From a cursed witch doctor he'd quickly become the esteemed *dokita*; at Sunday mass, the catechists even announced his arrival so as many people as possible would attend his consultations. His needs for extra personnel were met; dignitaries sent their sons to serve as interpreters, or as nurse's assistants. Notables sent him porters, and some even offered their daughters as wives or cooks for Jamot's health auxiliaries. All of this served to spread modern European medicine throughout our country.

"As for me, the call came in 1925. By some miracle, I managed to escape from two or three forced marriages, and that contributed to my success at school, where I tried to learn everything I could. But as an accomplished young woman, I just sat around the chief's compound with nothing to do, since I couldn't teach or work in the administration like my male cousins. Then one day Jamot himself came to suggest that my uncle send me to Ayos, where he was trying to set up a medical college. The doctor was so persuasive that my uncle agreed on the spot, provided Jamot promised to watch over me personally. And that he did.

"The next day, Jamot took me to Ayos, putting me in lodging not far from the health center and the medical school, in the hut of a woman, about twenty-five, who was the biggest coquette in the neighborhood. She was the only woman in the village to have a pagne with a matching scarf, and on Sundays she put on a pair of earrings, a bracelet, and a necklace—all machine made—and went to the Catholic church. People thought she was the mistress of my godfather, the doctor, and since she later gave birth to a little mixed-race girl, now almost everyone thinks that's true. Even me—I'm pretty convinced, but maybe I'm wrong. There were other white doctors around there.

"At nineteen I found myself there, in a white apron, ready to train to be a nurse, in the facility that would become the Instructional Center. What I learned there turned me into a different person; I'll always be grateful to Dr. Jamot. It wasn't easy for me at the start, especially during visits to neighboring villages for hands-on training, because some patients refused to allow a woman to palpate their ganglions. But the doctors who trained us—de Marqueissac, Montestruc, Chambon, and Le Rouzic—always knew what to say to help me do my best. In the end, I was recognized as an expert in lumbar punctures. I even learned suboccipital punctures, which, as you know, are acrobatic feats, to say the least. Before being allowed to take fluid samples, I had to prove myself in diagnostics—recognizing the symptoms of a wide range of ailments, giving shots, and analyzing blood and lymph samples. I put my heart into everything, even simple tasks like triage, filling out health histories, sterilizing tools, et cetera. The more I learned about a nurse's work, the more dedicated I became to the profession.

"But, more than just my studies, I loved our community life. In Ayos there were whites from many parts of France and Blacks from different Cameroonian tribes. What I learned from our differences was the most important part of my education—it's what makes me a privileged person. I met Catholics, Protestants, atheists, and pagans of both races with whom I got along, quarreled, and sometimes made peace. Before seeing me as a medical assistant, a lot of people treated me as women are treated wherever they're from. Some were ready to work toward equality, provided it was in an intimate moment in a bedroom or behind some bushes. Others would only do so with people like themselves. But most of the time, we worked things out together and, after a few compromises to balance out racism and tribalism, peace reigned. It was because of that cultural effervescence that we were able to put up with the monotony of our repetitive tasks, which sometimes made us feel like we were going in circles. For a girl like me, straight from her village, it was amazing. If I told you about everything I gained and lost through my collaboration with the white doctors at the Instructional Center, we'd be here for two days. I lost my virginity, and I gained so much from my reading. I won't elaborate on that first point. As for the second, I'm grateful to Dr. Monier's wife, Madeleine, who first put a novel in my hands.

"In 1927, when the Moniers arrived in Ayos for a monthlong training, I had long since completed my studies and was working alongside Dr. Henri de Marqueissac. In addition to serving as director of the Instructional Center, he also ran the clinic, which served people from all the surrounding areas. I immediately hit it off with Madeleine, a cultivated woman two years older than myself, who'd left her whole life behind in France to follow her husband to Africa. She brought a big trunk that contained more books than clothes, and spent her days leaning against a palm tree in the Center's courtyard, reading and writing. She quickly noticed I was the only woman on the medical staff and befriended me. We became inseparable. She talked to me about France, fashion, the world, and in return, I told her about local tribes, their customs, taboos, and legends. She was interested in everything; she even asked to accompany the medical units on their visits. Sadly, there were still villages that were off-limits to European women. Before Madeleine, I'd only read what my teachers wrote on a blackboard, and a few handwritten notes from my uncle, the chief. She offered me a brand-new book, *Raboliot*, suggesting that I read five pages a day. The next morning I told her the whole story, and she realized I'd spent the night reading to the end by the light of a hurricane lamp. It's by Maurice Genevoix—I'm sure you've read it, no?"

"Um . . . yes."

"I've since read many others, but that one is still my favorite. I take it with me everywhere. Besides reading and writing, Madeleine loved to sew. She showed me how to turn a pagne into a sheath or a flowing dress, and I treasure the sewing kit she left for me.

"When her husband finished his training and they were sent to Bafia, where he'd been named head of the health subdivision, Madeleine spoke with de Marqueissac and then wrote to Dr. Jamot, asking that I be assigned to the same health center. Jamot, not just accommodating, but truly aware of the difficult conditions his personnel worked under and attentive to their well-being, agreed. That's how I ended up here. My friend Madeleine also arranged for me to be lodged in the Moniers' residence. When we arrived, in November 1927, the subdivision of Bafia had seven preventive units on the ground, all led by health auxiliaries. Since then, the number has grown to ten. I knew some of the agents from the Instructional Center in Ayos, which has always been the hub for mission personnel. There was one member of the team I spent a good deal of time with during his training in Ayos. I'm sure you've heard of him—François Bertignac.

"Dr. Monier's first inspection revealed the region's catastrophic health conditions and horrifying statistics. The infection rate was close to 30 percent in some villages, and in others, there were almost no healthy adults. A man of action, Monier began by reorganizing his team. The subdivision has seventeen villages, so he assigned two to each health auxiliary. He decided to take the remaining three, closest to the main village, where he also staffed the health center. He dedicated one day a week to each village and spent the rest of his time at the health center. The unit he led included four nurses, including me, a secretary-interpreter, and two porters. As part of the unit, I accompanied Dr. Monier on all of his tours in the past two years. That's when I first came to Donenkeng; I came along when he examined a group of patients with sleeping sickness.

"In fact, a sixty-year-old patient with sleeping sickness from Donenkeng had already been brought to us. A desperate case. He was emaciated—like a corn stalk—anemic, with swollen eyes and monstrous ganglions. This patient, they said, needed special care, since he was the chief of Donenkeng. Monier treated him, following the usual protocol.

We kept watch over this important man for weeks, but there was no improvement, no response to the treatment. Dr. Monier persisted in caring for him. I don't know how, but one day, the old man was declared cured. And you could see that he was: he'd regained weight, he had energy and appetite, and all symptoms of the disease had disappeared. Even his blood—I drew the samples and tested them myself—was normal. This cure was celebrated by everyone. Dr. Monier decided to bring all the critical cases from the surrounding villages to Donenkeng, where he prescribed the same treatment that worked with the old chief. Seeing how quickly the patients responded, he gathered the health auxiliaries and told them to start using this new treatment everywhere in the subdivision.

"As the nurse in charge of the clinic for Dr. Monier's unit, I was often sent to the three villages in our area to check on patients who'd been given injections. Sometimes I traveled alone, with just one porter. The villagers were used to me. I was welcomed warmly and it wasn't uncommon for me to be invited to share a bowl of *kepen*, the local couscous, or for someone to give me some game to take with me. Madeleine came along when she could, and we'd talk about the love stories in books, or take cuttings from wildflowers, because she was planting flowers in the health center's courtyard.

"One afternoon I was giving a shot to the old chief of Donenkeng in his living room when a young man came in. I'd never seen him before, even though I'd been in the chief's compound several times. As soon as I set eyes on him, I felt self-conscious, as if I were badly dressed and my hair all wrong. Yet beneath my white apron I wore a short dress I'd sewn myself under Madame Monier's watchful eye. That morning I'd braided my hair into two long braids that showed off my brow, and I was even wearing shoes. I quickly breathed into my hand to check that my breath was still fresh, as was normal, since I'd brushed my teeth that morning with a twig of *mbomboye* that still had its bark and green leaves. When the old man howled because I'd pushed too hard on the syringe, I felt even more uncomfortable. I darted my eyes to the side, saw how the young man was staring at me, and quickly turned back to my injection. He left without saying a word. Before leaving the village with my porter, after seeing my last patient, I checked around the courtyard, but he was nowhere to be seen; I thought I must have dreamed him.

"At the health center where we lived, there was an enclosure that had been turned into a bathroom—just for Dr. and Madame Monier. A *boy* made sure the big basin was always filled with water. Of all the Blacks there, I was the only one Madeleine allowed to use the bathroom. You see, that shows that she was really my friend. Still, I preferred to bathe at the stream because you didn't have to rinse the water away and there were always plenty of *mbomboye* twigs to clean your teeth as much as you wanted. Look, there's one here . . .

"That evening I was coming back alone from the stream when the young man from the chief's compound stepped out from behind a tree in front of me. My first reaction was to cry out in fear. He held out his hands, gesturing for me to be calm, and said: 'My name is Abouem,' in French. I don't know who took the first step toward the other. But I do know that when we were close enough, I kissed him on the lips, just like a white man had kissed me for the first time in Ayos. He reacted as I had then: he backed up, confused. He wasn't familiar with that way of doing things, though it was normal for people like Madeleine and her husband. I kissed him again, and, so as to not upset him further, I let him do what he knew how to do. I'd had two or three adventures before that. Besides the first, which left a memory I'd rather forget, those dalliances had been a means of release. I'd never thought about being possessive of a man, much less being possessed by anyone at all. But when I saw Abouem the next day, I was sure I had found the man of my life, and since then, I live only for him.

"Of course, I talked about my affair with Madeleine. She asked to meet him, which wasn't hard to arrange since Abouem hung around the health center each evening. She thought he was handsome, but also pointed out that he'd be even better if he combed his hair and smiled more. She also warned that it would be up to me to teach him all the little things that would make him a big man in the country, since the metropole was starting to look for presentable natives.

"Before Abouem, I'd only thought about my work; meeting him brought balance to my life. As soon as I took off the white apron, I'd run to find my lover, who wasted no time taking off my short dress. I think we did a complete tour of all the bushes in Bafia trying to keep our romance secret. I made sure my friend Madeleine understood the importance of keeping this affair quiet, and, besides her, no one ever saw us together. Rumors spread fast here, and custom allows deceived husbands and the parents of rejected young girls to call for a palaver and seek reparations on the basis of rumor alone. Our favorite bush was about half a kilometer from the health center on the trail leading to the chief's compound, overlooking a stream. Between embraces, we also shared ideas. I told him about all the things I'd learned from my uncle and in books. He told me about his time at the boarding school in Doumé, and his frustration at being unable to continue his studies without spending several years in Europe—he wouldn't consider that. As the younger son, he was relieved he didn't have to prepare to take over from his father, because that let him focus on his own dreams. He wanted to go to Yaoundé, Brazzaville, Ubangi-Shari, and French West Africa, and bring together educated young natives to denounce colonization. He was passionate about it. I didn't share his dream, because I felt that when Abouem would have to choose between his project and me, I'd lose. I loved him and wanted to live with him, and for that to happen, I needed him to stay here. And providence came to my rescue.

"It took me a while to realize I was pregnant. It was my first time and I wasn't sure about things. My period was several weeks late, but only when the nausea started did I understand. I wasn't really all that surprised, given how much time we spent in the bushes. I waited a month, and when I was certain, I opened my heart to Abouem as we were leaving the bush one evening. He was so thrilled he jumped for joy, but even that news couldn't fully erase the unfamiliar melancholy air that had surrounded him all evening. I backed him into an acacia tree and demanded an explanation. He told me his father, the old chief, had lost his sight two days before. After expressing sympathy, I suggested he take the old man to the health center so that Dr. Monier could examine him. And he did. The old chief's blindness didn't surprise anyone much; as you know, old people often don't have good eyesight. Abouem and I tried to find a way around the merciless tradition that would deprive him of his status as father as soon as the notables of my clan heard about my growing belly. Thinking ahead, I sewed myself a loose, flowing dress. Before the end of that month, a second case of blindness was discovered in Donenkeng, then a third, and one in Lablé, and two more in Bitang.

"Soon the whole medical team was on edge. The mobile units found so many cases of blindness in the villages, all among people who'd been treated for sleeping sickness and declared cured. Trained as a native nurse, I'll admit I lacked the scientific background to understand what factors might have led to the catastrophe I was witnessing—in which I was even complicit. Yet intuition and a bit of common sense convinced me that our needles were the source of the problem. I couldn't sleep. It would be hard to find anyone in this subdivision who'd given more shots than I had. I loved my job—it gave me pride and satisfaction. Seeing a child, who'd been given up for dead before coming to me for treatment, tumbling through the grass, I felt like an angel doing good deeds. In truth, being a nurse isn't just a job, it's really doing God's work. I've understood that since my very first tour. I'd never imagined such a noble pursuit could lead to disaster. And I don't understand why Dr. Monier continued giving the same treatment. Nor can I explain why the ten health auxiliaries never tried to do anything—since they were certainly better trained than I. The fact is, in the months that followed, the number of cases of blindness in the villages kept growing, the medical units continued their circuits, never stopped giving injections. And Dr. Monier himself never missed one visit to Donenkeng.

"My pregnancy followed its course, and as months went by, to my great relief, I barely had a belly! At seven months, you'd have had to catch me bathing in the stream and look really closely to have any idea. And no one did. As soon as I put my loose dress back on, nothing gave me away. Besides Abouem, no one knew. Not even my friend Madeleine suspected a thing. This pregnancy was the only thing I ever hid from her. When Dr. Jamot arrived for his inspection tour, we spoke for a long time, I answered all his questions, and he left, still with no idea. I have a cousin in Yaoundé who was just the same; she lived in a hut with her father, mother, and brothers. The family only found out she was pregnant the day people came to get them because their daughter had given birth on the shore of the Mfoundi, where she'd gone to bathe. They needed a whole long palaver at the chief's compound for her mother to prove to her father she wasn't their daughter's accomplice. My plan was to do my cousin one better: to give birth without my family knowing and hide the baby from them. And I had another idea, I would find my baby's father a job that would keep him here. Until I could come up with something better, and since Abouem seemed set on revolution, I told him all the ideas I'd come up with about what had caused blindness in his father and all around the subdivision of Bafia. Such an accusation, coming from the nurse who'd inoculated his father with the poison herself, might've had the opposite effect and thwarted my own interests. I took the risk and luck was on my side, more than I'd even hoped. The day after my revelation, the old chief of Donenkeng died, preceded by his elder son, Abouem's brother. And we know what happened after that."

"I'm appalled!"

"Why? It would have happened sooner or later, with or without my contribution. The Bafias may be illiterate, idol-worshipping bushmen, but they still would have connected the blind people with the medical units. And the rebellion would have followed, no matter what, with Abouem or someone else at the lead. Seven hundred blind people all at once in an area with just seventeen villages—do you really think people wouldn't notice?"

"It's terrible!"

"True."

"There's something I don't understand. Several people now have told me about the start of the rebellion in Donenkeng. You're barely mentioned. How is that?"

"Well, I wasn't supposed to go to Donenkeng that day. I was almost at term, and my pregnancy was beginning to weigh on me, even though I managed to keep it secret. As far as anyone knew, I was just sick. Le Toullec, the health auxiliary filling in for Dr. Monier, had me replaced by a nurse named Mongui. I planned to get to Donenkeng the following day, whatever it took, and none of my coworkers suspected a thing. In fact, a few days before, Abouem and I had let his former wet nurse in on the secret. She's a traditional midwife, and was going to take care of me, giving me enemas with medicinal herbs to prepare me for childbirth. Everything was set, she even showed me the hut she had ready.

"Then came the fateful day when everything fell apart. I was resting in my bedroom in the health center when, about an hour after the medical unit had left, I started to feel better. I got up, put a smile on my face, and managed to convince Le Toullec to let me go take my post in Donenkeng. It was just a spur-of-the-moment decision to go early. I knew Abouem wouldn't wait much longer to start the uprising, but things were working out, which I took as a good omen. Just before I got to Donenkeng, I heard people crying, and it was chaos by the time I arrived in the village. That's everything."

"So, now all we have to do is escape from this fire trap—from the flames you fanned."

"Before Abouem and his followers set fire to the health center, I made him promise to save Madeleine Monier's garden, to spare the flowers from their anger. I hope he kept his word. I couldn't bear it if everything my friend has done was ruined. A week or two from now, as soon as I'm able, I'll go see that everything is as it should be."

"So you're refusing to leave with me?"

"*Akié!* Are you *trying* to not understand? Even if I wanted to, I couldn't."

"Why?"

"The moment I step outside of this village, Bertignac is a dead man. He is hiding in my hut as we speak, with no way out."

🦋

Night had fallen. Edoa and Damienne had left the *marigot* and had gone their separate ways.

In the courtyard the bonfires had been lit and the glow from the flames falling across ebony bodies dripping with sweat made the village look like the set of a horror show. Of course, the shadowed corners would serve Damienne well. She reconsidered the situation. There was no way to convince Edoa to return, so Chief Atangana's attack was unavoidable, the redhead Provat was about to start shooting, and Abouem was ready for a fight. In short, there was no way to avoid chaos. It was no longer time to play savior, it was time to flee. Dr. Jamot would understand. So far, so good. Thanks to Administrator Cournarie, Damienne could move freely until dawn. With a little luck and a lot of determination, that would give her enough time to make it past the Yambassa village; the Yambassa chief with his too-big clown shoes was still hanging around, filled with wine and kola, along with the miserable witch doctor and his headdress of grass and feathers. To ease her conscience, Damienne had agreed to see Bertignac before denouncing the redhead to Cournarie and fleeing. As long as her Pygmy guide remained faithful to her, she felt pretty good about this plan. Her primary fear, other than a native uprising, was that Cournarie and Pouget would take off and leave her behind.

When she returned, they were still sitting in the living room, and clearly angry. The ever-diplomatic administrator berated Damienne severely, in a carefully restrained voice and without ever losing his smile, in case they were being watched. Backed by the gendarme, Cournarie said they must leave Donenkeng immediately, which led the young woman to suspect his plot to manipulate the chiefs had failed.

Buying time, Damienne said she had something important to tell him. Cournarie glared at her suspiciously, and insisted she tell him immediately. Weighing her various secrets, she revealed that Edoa was in a hut at the back of the chief's compound. Since the beginning, she'd balked at explaining why she was there, since Jamot shouldn't seem to be worried about the safety of just one native nurse. To her surprise, Cournarie and Pouget barely reacted. They merely exchanged glances and signaled that she should leave them alone.

The courtyard was crowded with people. Edoa was in her hut, along with the traditional midwife, who was caring for the baby. Since the baby's birth she came to the hut at least four times a day to attend the mother and baby, bring meals, or collect laundry. Sometimes for no reason at all. Just then she was cleaning the baby's belly button, without the slightest idea that a white man was lying on the ground under the bed. When she finished, the midwife would go across the courtyard to her own hut, on the other side of the path. Then the way would be clear for Damienne, who was keeping watch and trying to imagine a way for Bertignac to escape. She waited several long minutes. The elder of the chiefs crouched down beside a bonfire, picked up a glowing ember with his hand, shoved it into his pipe, and went back to join the other guests under the shelter. Focused on avoiding the Yambassa chief, who was waving his arms about wildly, she almost missed the midwife who had already crossed the courtyard, sidled behind the balafon players who'd joined the drummers, and was about to cross the trail. The path was clear. Damienne hurried to the living room and rushed past Cournarie and Pouget, who just stared as she slipped back into the chief's compound.

Inside the hut, Damienne pulled the screen into place. It was dark. Edoa was on the bed nursing her baby. A hurricane lamp on the floor, its globe half-black with soot, cast long shadows. The young woman stayed silent for a moment, then, without looking away from her baby, she knocked on the bamboo bed frame. Silence. A light rustling, and then, between the bed and the back wall, a blond head appeared. François Bertignac struggled to sit up, and despite the poor light, Damienne sensed panic in his eyes. He started crying.

Damienne motioned for him to approach. Leaning against the wall, he walked toward her, dragging one foot. He had spent the last eight days lying beneath a makeshift bed. His ankle was hurt, and he was as silent as if he were already dead. A broken man. She couldn't abandon him there. He leaned on the young woman's shoulder. She pulled the screen open and a welcome breeze filled the room. Damienne took a deep breath and held it, because Bertignac stank. She dragged the poor man behind the huts and down toward the *marigot*. She couldn't ask the Pygmy for help—he was in the courtyard celebrating. The stress was overwhelming; Damienne felt like she was losing her mind. At the corner of the hut, she looked left and caught a glimpse of the courtyard filled with laughing people. She wondered if those natives could see the two white shadows slipping off in the darkness. One thing was sure: if anyone did notice, it was all over. Happily, the forest was close and the fugitives were soon safe beneath the trees. You could barely see a meter ahead, and for once, that was a plus. Feeling their way along, breaking the delicate buds from shrubs to mark their trail, they advanced slowly, sometimes tripping over a log or a rock. Soon she felt the soft dirt of the *marigot* beneath their feet. A gentle flapping of wings made Damienne jump as something passed close by her head: a bat. Bertignac washed his face. Damienne took a deep breath and asked, "Bertignac, why are you still in this damned village? Everyone thought you'd escaped!"

"I never made it out of Donenkeng. I wouldn't even be alive except that Edoa saved me when I was running for my life, with the whole village on my heels."

"Tell me."

"It started on a Saturday . . . But, what day is it today?"

"It's Sunday—December 15, 1929."

"Ah . . . Well, that Saturday, I almost lost my life. A mob of natives, mad as hell, armed with tools, was chasing me. By some miracle I managed to escape from a group of women with clubs, and I was running toward the chief's compound. My only hope was to slalom between the huts, reach the forest before my assailants, and somehow hide. The natives are more comfortable than I am in the bush, it was a slim hope at best, but I had no choice. Rushing between two huts, I ran right into Edoa, and she quickly pointed to a door. Seconds later, I heard her urging my pursuers into the forest. They dove into the bush, shrieking war cries.

"Inside, I fell flat on the ground. My heart was pounding, my temples were on fire, I couldn't breathe, I thought I was going to hyperventilate. I couldn't think straight—too many thoughts raced through my head. I couldn't even manage to drag myself to the back of the hut when I saw people passing on the other side of the screen. It was a group of mourners, about a dozen women standing outside chatting. They were no more than a meter away, going on about just what they'd do when they caught me. I was still gasping for breath, trying to swallow and inhale at the same time. Then I started to choke, and fought not to cough or even exhale too loudly. The whole time I kept my eyes fixed on the screen, as if to magically keep it shut; all it would take was a gust of wind or an awkward shoulder to knock it down. The 'Ave Maria' started running through my mind—though I haven't been to church in at least fifteen years. How long did I lie there and pray? Suddenly the screen gave a sharp crack, and my newfound religion was lost again. My pulse raced, I jumped and crawled away from the door. It was Edoa, though that did nothing to relax me. She whispered for me to hide beneath the bed, and I did. It wasn't exactly comfortable, but it was a place to hide. I mustered what little lucidity remained and tried to come up with answers to some questions.

"Why was Edoa there? What was she doing in Donenkeng? She'd been sick in bed in the health center and Mongui had had to take her place. Strange things happen in Africa, but it was too much to understand how Edoa could be in two places at the same time! In any case, I owed her my life, and I hoped she would continue to protect me until nightfall, when I could try to escape. I wondered why she seemed to have her own hut and wasn't threatened by the villagers. And what had happened to our medical supplies? And the rest of my unit? I started worrying about the other members of my unit, then remembered how quickly they'd distanced themselves from me. I couldn't remember seeing a single nurse being chased, though there was a whole horde of attackers. As I replayed the sequence of events, Edoa paced from one side of the hut to the other. I could only see her feet, but she was the only native in the region who always wore shoes. Outside, the mourners still hadn't gotten ahold of themselves, and neither had the talkative women. Since I couldn't hear anything coming from the main courtyard, that meant the village men, under Abouem's orders, were still chasing me. I prayed for night to fall.

"Suddenly I saw two feet at the end of the bed. They were women's feet, but not Edoa's. An older woman's. Since I hadn't seen her come in, I concluded I'd fallen asleep or passed out. I had no idea what time it was, but thanks to the cracks at the bottom of the wall in front of me, I could tell it was still daylight. The feet shuffled along the side of the bed. And the bed was occupied, the frame creaked terribly. It sounded like she was getting a massage. When the old woman stepped back, two other feet appeared. Even bare, I recognized them right away. The two women left the hut. I tried to shift my position, but my ankle hurt unbearably. My whole back ached and I was sweating bullets. I couldn't catch my breath, it felt like I was being buried alive, but knowing what waited outside gave me the strength to stay put. Nevertheless, it took all my self-control not to lose my mind. When Edoa came back, the old feet were still with her; the woman set down a big bowl of food and another of water almost right in front of my nose. It was *kepen*—an amazing corn couscous that people around here eat with all sorts of different sauces. There's no Bafia without *kepen*. The two women arranged a time to meet later that evening and the old woman left. Edoa knocked on the bed and I poked my head out. She told me I'd been snoring and advised me to lie on my stomach. She warned that she'd say she'd been attacked if anyone found me in her hut. We shared the *kepen* and egusi bean sauce, and then I went back to my hiding place. Lying on my stomach was even more uncomfortable, and soon I had a face full of dirt. I started to despair. I had such bad luck! In four years I'd had so many adventures in Africa, I'd shared so much with the people, and now a simple mistake had ruined everything just two weeks before I was to go home. Two weeks! I was mad as hell. Other, darker thoughts filled my mind, passing the time till dusk. When the old woman came back, I paid closer attention to what she and Edoa said. I couldn't believe my ears!

"Still, I didn't laugh, I know how good the midwives are. Their standards of cleanliness may leave much to be desired, but those women are not clowns. They're wise, true midwives, and have been working here for thousands of years. They know a lot about giving birth. Their collection of medicines—and I admit I've been interested in them for some time now—is impressive for the quality of their antibiotic decoctions and strengthening tonics. African midwives are a true cultural treasure, and we could learn a lot by studying their methods. According to the old woman, Edoa was not just pregnant, she was almost full term. The village matron thought she'd have the baby in no more than four days!

"No one but Edoa could've pulled one over on a whole health center like that. A doctor, an armada of health auxiliaries, nurses, even Madeleine Monier, who certainly didn't seem like a fool to me. To be pregnant and make it to full term without any of the health professionals around having the slightest idea was really something. That's when I realized Edoa was deserting us, and that she'd planned it all. There was only one logical conclusion: she'd decided to stay in Donenkeng with the man responsible for her pregnancy. Given where we were, it could only be Abouem. Female duplicity isn't anything new, but some women make it almost an art. Another way of looking at my situation was that I was caught in a mousetrap, at the mercy of my tormentor's companion. Maybe she wasn't intending to give me up to her man—a gift in addition to the baby—but I couldn't be sure. Whatever the case might be, I needed to get out of there. Unfortunately, when night fell, I couldn't leave. I'd taken a blow to my ankle and it was swollen. My foot hurt so much that I couldn't put any weight on it.

"My first night under Edoa's bed was the worst of my life. Claustrophobia alone was torment enough, but on top of that, my right foot was throbbing, I was afraid that if I fell asleep, I'd snore, or that Abouem might suddenly appear at his beloved's door, or that I might simply be betrayed. I didn't shut my eyes the whole night, and I wasn't alone; the singing and wailing in the village's main courtyard didn't let up until dawn. It was a wake for the old chief and his son, who were to be buried later that day.

"Because of the double burial, dignitaries from neighboring villages flooded into Donenkeng. From morning to night, people came and went in all directions. Not exactly the best conditions for an escape. Before the midwife came to care for Edoa, I gently rapped on the bedframe. When Edoa peeked down, I showed her my foot. It was swollen to twice its size. She left the hut. When she came back with the medical kit, I whispered she was taking a risk that could catch the eye of an attentive villager and cost me dearly. Edoa explained that her status and condition were known to everyone in the village, which made her beyond question. And besides, she'd told them the medical kit was needed for her own care. That seemed reasonable. She gave me a shot that I'm sure saved my foot. That day, and the next, the midwife gave her several doses of honey. It was pouring rain when the baby was born on the fourth day, just as the midwife had predicted. It completely convinced me of her wisdom. There beneath the bamboo bed, I lived through all the stages of labor; I heard the ululations, saw with my own eyes the blood-drenched placenta wrapped in a banana leaf. Births may be exceptional moments that distract us from the vicissitudes of this world, but hearing the baby's first cries, I still couldn't help thinking of my friend Pouget, who had now surely lost Edoa forever."

"What do you mean?" Damienne said with a start.

"Before meeting Abouem, Edoa was engaged to the chief gendarme, Pouget—he was madly in love with her."

"Pouget? No, I don't believe it, that can't be."

"Believe it. I'm the one who brought them together and tried to help patch things up when they started to go wrong.

"I met Edoa four years ago, in Ayos. I'd just gotten off the boat from France, and my training coincided with the start of her studies. Before I really noticed how beautiful she was, I was struck by the charisma of a native woman who could speak up for herself. It was a miracle she was even there, really, with all those men and talking about medicine. Not just happy to be there, she was bold, she thought for herself. And she didn't just defend her ideas, she distilled them, as if she had nothing to prove to anyone. Compared to her native brothers in the same classes, the contrast was stark. They smiled, watching everything they said, doing whatever it took to please, believing everything they were told, and disparaging each other to make themselves look better. They imitated their trainers without asking the slightest question, much less expressing their own point of view. The only thing they agreed on was that she was to blame for not keeping in her place. They were furious because she got the best grades in the school, always top of the class. But Edoa, she paid them no mind. During the two months I was there, I never saw anyone put that girl in her place. She determined where she should be and, without any fanfare, stood her ground. Really, she wasn't doing anything extraordinary; she just said no when a suggestion didn't suit her, and yes when it did. But she stood out, because that's not how things usually are.

"Two years later, I was thrilled to see Edoa at the health center in Bafia. I was already established in the area; I'd made friends among all the tribes and among the whites as well. Pouget, the gendarme, was my closest friend. We had so much in common; like me, he's from Auvergne, is single, and plays the guitar. When you end up in the same village at the end of the world, that practically makes you related.

"Pouget wanted Edoa from the first moment he saw her. Here, white men usually think they're doing a native woman a favor by chasing her, and usually the women don't tell them any different. So Pouget was pretty confident, cocky even, when he made his move on Edoa. She wanted nothing to do with him. She met his rudeness with a calm pride that knocked him back and transformed his desire into passion. For weeks, he felt like a fool. When he realized I was friends with Edoa, he insisted I arrange a meeting. She was open to it, provided he apologized, and it seems Pouget did, because they became lovers. Pouget didn't hide much from me. He planned to take Edoa to France. He knew his parents would disapprove of the woman he'd chosen to marry, but he loved her, and was prepared to give everything up for her, even if it meant spending the rest of his life in Africa. He would have done it, too, if Abouem hadn't come on the scene.

"I don't know how everything played out, because I wasn't always there. But one day, I came out of the bush for supplies and found Pouget transformed, no longer the dapper man I'd sung bawdy songs with in the canteen, like 'C'est si bon quand c'est défendu.' He told me Edoa had ended things without warning, and for the past three weeks, all his attempts to speak with her had failed. Madame Monier had tried, but even she had no luck. Poor fellow was so upset that I finally believed his love was sincere and promised to find out what I could. At the health center, I was greeted by a radiant Edoa. The reason she'd ended things was plain to see, though she tried to convince me otherwise. Lying through her teeth, she said she needed to think more seriously about her life, and so on. She asked me to tell Pouget she was sorry. My curiosity piqued, I snooped around, and it didn't take long to identify the stallion responsible. When I saw them together, my first thought was that Edoa had found a man worthy of her. But mostly I thought this was the start of Pouget's troubles. I decided not to tell him who his rival was because, knowing how smitten he was and that he was armed, I feared he might do something stupid."

"Did Pouget ever learn who Edoa left him for?"

"Not that I know."

"And if he were to learn now, how do you think he'd react?"

"Hard to say. But seeing what Abouem is capable of, I'm glad I kept the truth from him. Pouget's still bitter, and I know he's calculating and vindictive; it's best for everyone that he stay in the dark."

"Bertignac, don't move. I'll be right back."

❦

Damienne was out of breath. Dr. Jamot trusted her, but not only had she proved incapable of bringing his goddaughter back, she'd possibly put her in danger. Pouget, her spurned and vengeful lover, was in the chief's compound, and thanks to Damienne and her naïveté, he knew Edoa was there, too, alone in a hut at the back, mostly hidden from view . . . Betrayed men are the last to know, but then comes a moment of realization when everything becomes crystal clear. And then they are ruthless beasts. And unless gendarme Pouget was a complete imbecile, he must have figured it out.

It was even darker on the path back up to the huts in the village. One misstep and she'd twist her ankle, or even worse. Damienne hurried nonetheless. Her fears had been focused on Chief Atangana's mission of revenge, then on the show of force planned by Provat and his gang, so she'd thought she had at least half a day before war broke out. Now she realized the primary security risk in Bafia had already infiltrated native headquarters. And that risk was named Pouget. Since the previous night Damienne had sensed something was off with the chief of the gendarmerie, an aloofness she'd taken for racism. She'd been wrong about that. Bertignac's story showed her a rejected man who was falling apart, projecting onto all the natives the mistrust and bitterness inspired by the woman who'd betrayed him. His mind clouded by jealousy, Pouget was in a position to provoke a catastrophe, without even realizing it. For once, Damienne hoped she was wrong.

She rushed out of the forest like a wild beast. Racing around the first huts, she thought she heard French coming from Edoa's hut. Raised voices. Damienne raced past, found the hallway, and tiptoed back to the living room. In the shadows she leaned against a screen, which crashed down loudly, but she didn't seem to notice. She was already in the living room—it was empty. Not even Cournarie. Without pausing, she raced into the courtyard. Everything was strangely silent, and it took her a moment to grasp what that meant.

When Damienne realized that she'd interrupted the solemn speech of the elder chief, all eyes were already on her. She saw Administrator Cournarie under the shelter with the chiefs, sitting between two dignitaries. He glared at her, but she wasn't sure why. In any event, she couldn't retreat now. That wasn't an option.

Abouem had already noticed the strange white woman wearing a pagne who never stayed still. When she'd greeted him, he'd been surprised by how tightly she clung to him. He'd kept his composure, like a true chief, but that hadn't kept him from wondering whether maybe . . . Of course, he was in love with Edoa, but that was a weakness he'd need to control, as the other chiefs had told him during the secret investiture ritual. That this woman might find him appealing was a surprise, unsettling even. Happily, he could take as many wives as he wished. The only problem was that everyone said that when a white woman has children with a native man, the children are lost to him from the start, because sooner or later she'll take them to Europe. And that would be a hell of a problem for Abouem. That's what he was thinking as he watched the white woman walk toward him. Curious, he ordered his guard to let her approach.

Feeling pressure rising, Damienne knelt down before Chief Abouem's wicker throne and said, "Majesty, Edoa is in danger. Please act quickly!"

Abouem froze and stared at her. His thoughts of infidelity flew away. He rose. With a nonchalant wave toward the chief's compound, he sent a contingent of well-built young men racing off. He didn't move. For two minutes, the silence was deafening.

Cournarie tried to make eye contact with Damienne, who did her best to avoid him—she didn't know what to think. She wondered if she'd made the right decision, or if she'd only acted in the interests of her own mission. A roar came from the back of the compound, bringing everyone in the courtyard to their feet. When gendarme Pouget appeared, surrounded by angry scowling natives, the village exploded with shouts. It took the intervention of the elder chief and a half dozen others to keep the gendarme from being mobbed right there. The remaining chiefs formed a circle around Cournarie and Damienne, because villagers were pointing at them. It was chaos, fights even broke out among the natives. The people's anger was legitimate, no doubt, but raffia wine probably played some part in their frenzy.

As the three whites were brought together behind a protective line of the area's traditional royalty, Damienne met the gendarme's gaze. He had, by some miracle, just escaped an awful death, and yet he seemed unbelievably calm. There was no way to explain it, unless he was already mad. He stared at her with half-closed eyes, one shut more than the other, lips slightly open, as if he was trying to smile. Besides him, no one in the village had any semblance of self-control, none of the Blacks and not the other two whites. Danger was everywhere.

Pouget's stare gave her goose bumps, and Damienne quickly understood her immediate threat. Now that Edoa was out of his reach, Pouget focused all the bitterness and frustration of these past months on her. Damienne no longer worried about the hysterical, shouting natives— she could turn her back on them, but not on Pouget.

Abouem lifted his baton and the crowd fell silent. He turned and looked at the colonial delegation, one by one. The scene may have appeared calmer, but the barely controlled violence was unbearable.

In the darkness of that steamy December night in 1929, in the heart of a region enflamed by a medical blunder that left seven hundred people blind, the Bafias crying for revenge suddenly fell silent to hear their chief's verdict. At the center were three whites, none of whom were responsible for the blunder. They were surrounded by thousands of glaring eyes and dark bodies barely visible in the glow of the wood fires. Chief Abouem began. In a controlled voice he declared that all persons of the white race found on his lands were his adversaries—other than Pouget and Bertignac, whom he considered his sworn enemies. He assured everyone that, so long as the three who'd been promised safe passage were in his village, not even a mosquito would harm them. Then his voice grew angry. He would give all the whites in Bafia until morning to cross the Mbam and Sanaga Rivers. Then, at dawn, they would attack the residence of the colonial administrator and chase down any stragglers who remained in the subdivision. His words were met by a chorus of war cries. The crowd spontaneously split in two, forming a double row. The whites had to go.

There was no more time for negotiations. The colonial delegation made its way along the human corridor, out toward the edge of the village. The drums rose up, sharp beats spreading out over the trees. Damienne turned back for one last look—not a single dancer was moving to the drums. They were disappointed they had to wait until morning to hunt down the whites. By allowing them to leave the village, Abouem had shown his benevolence, though his actions amounted to releasing pigeons in a shooting competition. They all knew the delay he'd accorded wasn't sufficient for them to get out of the subdivision. At best it was a head start that gave them just a glimmer of hope for survival, for those fearsome hunters were experts with stone axes and spears. On top of that, the tom-toms, no longer for dancing, spread the news to all the other villages.

The Europeans in Bafia were now on their own, and it would be at least four days before anyone could come to their aid. Each could rely only on his own legs. As for Damienne, she had one last hope: she knew Ndongo the Pygmy wouldn't abandon her.

But then, there was Bertignac. Damienne had gotten him out of his hiding place, where, though he'd been in uncomfortable and dirty conditions, at least he could have possibly held out a few more weeks. If she abandoned him by the *marigot*, where he was waiting for her, she condemned him to death: he'd be found and killed before daybreak. With everything the angry crowd in Donenkeng blamed on him, he couldn't even hope for a dignified death. And the path to Yaoundé was long and difficult; making it there was a feat even in the best of conditions—for Bertignac, impossible. Reason dictated that Damienne give up on him, especially since no one, besides Edoa, knew she'd seen him. And Edoa didn't matter anymore. Beyond her own conscience, nothing connected Damienne Bourdin to François Bertignac.

They made it past the last house in the village and plunged into darkness. They could still see fires glowing in the courtyard and shadows moving about. Damienne hoped no one was following them, other than Ndongo, who must be on their trail, discreet as ever. She was already trying to figure out how to lose her companions and join him. But, even though she'd come to her senses and was obsessively focused on getting away from Bafia, she couldn't bear the guilt that would weigh on her shoulders for the rest of her days. She decided to tell Cournarie the truth about Bertignac, certain the pragmatic administrator would decree without hesitation that the health auxiliary had to be sacrificed. Damienne just needed someone else to make that decision so she could sleep peacefully. And Cournarie was surely used to summary executions—he was a colonial administrator, after all.

Cournarie yelled so much that Damienne was relieved when he ordered her to cut through the woods to find Bertignac. The administrator gave her thirty minutes; if she wasn't back by then, she should consider herself on her own. Damienne was almost through the first row of bushes when she heard Pouget offer to go with her. She couldn't refuse. Bertignac was his close friend, and it was to the gendarme's credit that he'd put himself in danger to give the health auxiliary a chance to survive. Besides, two of them would have an easier time transporting an injured man.

Cournarie hid behind a tree to the side of the trail. Damienne led the way because she knew where Bertignac was; Pouget followed behind. Once past the bushes at the edge of the trail, the forest was big trees and not a lot of underbrush. They could make their way fairly easily around the saplings—the main challenge being that it was almost totally dark. Of all the dangers, the one Damienne feared the most was right behind her, not snakes she might step on or thorns or wasp nests hanging at head height. Orienting herself relative to the huts in the village, she headed in a direction that should lead them downstream; then they'd just need to follow the bank.

Damienne's enchanted childhood in Marseille seemed like a distant memory. All her failings, the privations during the war, the poverty of her life with Samuel in that dreadful studio on the rue du Sar in Sète, her failure at the newspaper, the editors' indifference, her brother-in-law's spite, her sister's cruelty, the crisis . . . All of that seemed like luxury compared to what she'd endured since she'd stepped foot in Cameroon, and in Bafia. A world that books might have given her some hint of, but she'd never imagined. The loss of her baby had been the worst thing in her life—she still wasn't over the pain. Edoa had put her finger right on that wound; Damienne's weak spot hadn't escaped her, and she knew just how to exploit it. But in Africa, Damienne had seen people suffer through far worse. Everything she'd seen in the past three weeks had changed her for good.

As soon as they were alone in the bush, Pouget leapt on Damienne. She'd been expecting something, but wasn't prepared for the fury he unleashed. Ndongo was right there. Damienne couldn't see what her guide was doing to the gendarme, but his cries were horrible. She called out Ndongo's name and screamed "No!" three times, hoping he'd spare

Pouget, if he hadn't already gouged out his eyes. Mostly, Damienne didn't want to lose her sense of direction in the chaos—it was easy enough to get lost in the forest in broad daylight. Damienne could barely make out the band of amulets on the Pygmy's arm, but she saw he was sitting astride his victim. In the dark, she couldn't tell what state the gendarme was in, but she thought it unlikely he had retained his remarkable calm.

It took effort to convince Ndongo to release him, but he finally agreed to let Pouget up. He helped Damienne and the gendarme reach the *marigot* as quickly as possible, then they headed upstream, calling for Bertignac. Damienne feared he'd already fled. Walking along the stream, they clearly heard the noises from the village, so he must have heard the earlier drama. She could still hear the tom-toms and, worse, a second drumbeat in the distance. They went on, calling his name. Damienne tripped on a huge rock half-submerged in the water. She didn't like the idea of abandoning Bertignac, but truth be told, part of her was happy to be rid of him. No one could say they hadn't tried. She turned and started back downstream. Instead of following her, Pouget continued calling "François! François!" Suddenly high in the trees they heard a voice and a rustling. Bertignac was there. Damienne appreciated his resourcefulness. His long stays among the natives had transformed him; he could hide from a Pygmy in the forest. For a moment, Damienne tried to imagine Abouem's reaction if he were to know that his two enemies were together just a stone's throw away—she shuddered at the thought of what he'd do. Meanwhile, the friends hugged and patted one another on the back; Damienne had to intervene so they would not go on forever. Cournarie was impatiently waiting for them, hidden behind his tree.

Once together on the side of the trail, they took stock of how their bad situation had gotten worse with the return of Bertignac. Three people had been accorded safe passage; now there were four of them. They didn't count the Pygmy, not out of racism, but because he was free to go wherever he wanted. They needed to make a decision. Cournarie didn't give the others a chance to make suggestions. He ordered the

gendarme to head straight to Yaoundé and ask Commissioner Marchand
to send a battalion of soldiers to put down the rebellion. That meant
Damienne and Bertignac would follow Cournarie to his residence, where
he intended to hole up and wait for reinforcements. As soon as he heard
his orders, Pouget gave his friend one last vigorous handshake and left.
A short time later, the others were back at the administrator's residence.

❧

Damienne's pagne was dirty and torn. The few remaining shreds were
plastered to her belly and thighs, and even though her companions in
hiding weren't giving her attributes a second glance, she wanted something more respectable to wear. Sikini was shocked—not even a native
woman could've still worn that pagne. To cheer her up, Damienne promised to replace it with white-women's clothes, and Sikini believed her.
Damienne's belted dress, which the girl had washed as well as possible,
wasn't much more than a rag. But Damienne was happy to have it back.

According to the clock, it was 11:48 p.m. No one was asleep. Everyone
was in the living room and they all knew what was coming. There were
eighteen people left in the residence, counting the Pygmy. Most of the
native nurses, clerks, and *boys* had fled, and no one could blame them.
Only three Blacks had chosen to stay, Bidias, Sikini, and Ndongo.

Ndongo chastised Damienne in his language. As soon as she was
dressed, he tied the belt of amulets that she'd forgotten around her
waist again. None of the whites had a chance to laugh, though, because
Cournarie had tasks for everyone, and they were all focused on what
they needed to do.

The plot hatched by Provat and his gang had dissolved before they'd
had a chance to act. They were all in this together. Once Cournarie
reviewed their situation, the redhead told everyone what he'd had in
mind before Damienne could denounce him. Damienne was *almost*
out of secrets. Now everyone knew about Edoa's duplicity, Bertignac

was back, and Provat's show of force had been voted down. Because Cournarie was so openly hostile to her, Damienne had even had to reveal her real mission just so he didn't lock her up. Cournarie now knew that, while she was actually a doctor, she'd been assigned to the health center in Sangmélima and come to Bafia on Dr. Jamot's orders to retrieve Edoa, whatever it took. The only thing she didn't disclose was the tribal war brewing between Paramount Chief Atangana's Ewondos and Chief Abouem's Bafias. There was no question now of Dr. Jamot's deadline being met. The coming battle was unavoidable.

Damienne regretted not having told Cournarie that earlier—it would've had an impact on negotiations in Donenkeng. Instead of trusting in diplomacy, she'd bet on Edoa's return, thinking all she needed to do to get her back was to find her. Now that it was too late, Damienne was afraid if she told him, she'd forever be the target of the administrator's ire. Yet it was still useful information, in the sense that it meant the siege would last for no more than three days. Three days, not the five they were planning for if the chief of the gendarmerie came back with reinforcements. They couldn't be sure that Pouget would make it to Yaoundé. But with Paramount Chief Atangana on his way, they only had to hold out for two days and then they'd watch from the window as the Ewondos massacred the Bafias. The Bafias might have shown they were ready for a fight, but Damienne had reason to put her money on an Ewondo victory.

That night, Bidias didn't need to worry about who would sleep where. With the dancing and war cries outside, no one was going to sleep at all.

❦

The first glimmers of dawn revealed a courtyard filled with Black bodies, as black as the heart of darkness. Abouem was a man of his word. He'd removed his ceremonial pagne and covered his bare chest with strands of beads. His face was daubed with the same colors as his warriors. If anyone holed up inside peeked out the window, they met the steely gaze of those outside, who now crowded close to the veranda. There was no way to know how many warriors were there—too many, to be sure— too many to have come from one village. An army composed of men in their twenties and thirties from all the villages in the subdivision; they'd come together quickly, united by the growing number of people blinded by tryparsamide. They answered each of Abouem's phrases as one, raising their spears and whooping. They were armed with machetes, clubs, and stone axes. No firearms were visible in their camp.

Inside, all the furniture had been moved to barricade the doors. Cournarie had dug up an additional rifle, which made four. Each bullet was precious—they had so few. The main façade had three wide windows; two weapons were aimed there, held by the redhead and a gendarme. Another was out back, in the kitchen. The remaining windows were guarded by unarmed people; their job was to call for backup if needed. The final weapon was in the hallway, to be used wherever needed. Damienne was posted at the middle window in the living room; from there she could look out over the whole courtyard. She watched as the first round of stones was thrown. They pounded on the shutters and roof, thundering madly. Happily, no breaches. That lifted spirits in the living room and, during the brief calm before the second round, Damienne reassured herself that the tide was turning in their favor: if the natives were trying to flush them out with stones, they could just sit back, cross their arms, and wait for reinforcements to arrive. Even without reserves of water and food, it was doable. Paramount Chief Atangana would be on his way soon.

Suddenly everything fell silent—no songs, no whoops. An unexpected and sinister silence. Then the post-office chief, stationed at a bedroom window, rushed into the living room in a swoon. Realizing he was having a heart attack, Damienne instinctively abandoned her post to provide aid. Others became hysterical. It was chaos until the redhead confirmed that no native had broken through the abandoned bedroom window, and someone else was assigned to guard it. There wasn't much to be done for the poor postman, other than making sure he could breathe and waiting until he could swallow aspirin. Peering out from her spot, Damienne saw the witch doctor Teketekete—easily recognizable because of his headdress of grass and feathers—at Abouem's side. She reasoned that all the traditional chiefs had come. Had they all rallied behind Abouem? Even the ones Cournarie manipulated? The ones who kept tearing down the others? Damienne's wonderings were stopped cold, because now she saw natives carrying pieces of wood. They were going to set fire to the residence, just as they had the health center. Administrator Cournarie had also seen. He called for Bidias, his faithful *boy*, and conferred quietly with him.

Two windows were thrown open and gunfire quickly followed. Abouem was right up front. Damienne saw him shudder, as if he were executing an elegant Bafia dance. For a moment, she thought he was invincible, dancing in place, absorbing all the bullets from both rifles. In slow motion, Abouem fell. Before hitting the ground, he managed to lift his scepter high in the air. A swarm of spears flew at the windows, and the battle was on. In the living room the shooters barely had time to duck; a horrible whistling filled the room, followed by thuds. Damienne saw the windows were still open! Too stunned to move, everyone froze where they'd crouched to hide.

When the spears stopped falling, Damienne lifted her head and peered out her still-closed window. The courtyard had thinned out. Two natives sat on the ground, one holding his arm, the other his thigh. No one paid attention to them—everyone had gathered around Abouem's body. Damienne tried to get a better look. She thought she saw a white beard, possibly the elder chief. But as she watched, to be sure, there was a whoop and two natives jumped through the open windows and into the living room, each armed with machetes. They were covered in sweat and smeared with war paint, eyes filled with rage; their appearance sent panic through the room—no one had had time to reload their weapons.

Some retreated along the hallway, chased by the first assailant, leaving only four white people in the room: the postmaster, splayed out on the floor; the two men with rifles, sitting against the wall below their windows; and Damienne. The second assailant turned toward her. When he lifted his machete, she thought her final hour had come. Then he turned away, as if he hadn't even seen her, and fell upon the redhead on her right. Provat tried to parry the blows with his rifle, but he was hit several times. A spectacle of pure savagery. Damienne fainted under the shock but, before she fell, she thought she saw the Pygmy coming across the living room toward the windows. Then everything went black.

Ndongo was proud of himself. What would've happened if he hadn't made sure the white woman put her grigri back on? He would have liked to tie a grigri around each white person in the house, but, alas! He didn't have enough amulets. And his assignment was to watch over that one white woman, not all the others. They could make do with their own cross-shaped grigris—he'd seen that some wore them around their necks. His charge had fainted. He shut the windows, so no more Bafias could come in. He didn't really know why the Bafias, who made such good couscous, had suddenly gotten so angry with the whites, but that wasn't his problem. First, the windows. He, Ndongo, could stand in front of the windows because he was in no danger.

🦋

Damienne woke up in hell. Four bodies lay around her. Both assailants were dead. Sikini was sobbing over Provat's body. The postmaster was lying nearby, and he was still breathing. All the windows were shut tight. All the survivors had gathered in the living room. The chief of schools had a horrible wound on his back that a health auxiliary was trying to stitch up; he'd taken a blow from a machete back in the hallway, before his aggressor was shot down. Everyone was trembling, except Ndongo, who was by Damienne's side.

Once again, the Pygmy spoke to her in his incomprehensible jargon, as if he were sure it was the lingua franca. As he spoke, he checked that Damienne's belt of amulets was securely tied. She recalled her recent brushes with death and remembered Ndongo explaining that his grigris would make her invisible to her enemies; the thought that she was playing with African witchcraft made her swoon. The stunted little man before her, who'd been her guide and was clearly convinced of his own invulnerability, believed what he said. Not once since she'd met him had he expressed any doubts. Even if he acted strangely, and his thinking was hard to follow, the results of his actions gave the force of logic to his words. And logic was something Damienne understood.

From that moment on, Damienne Bourdin also believed she was invulnerable and decided her ridiculous grigri would never leave her.

Now fully alert, Damienne rushed to the windows. Outside, the natives also looked uncertain. Abouem's death was a blow to those young men who now wandered around his remains like so many orphaned chicks. Off to one side, several of the traditional chiefs, including the elder, were arguing. Damienne turned to Cournarie. She suggested he send out his *boy* Bidias to request a meeting with the elder of the Bafia chiefs. To convince the administrator he had a good chance of succeeding in these new negotiations, Damienne told him that Paramount Chief Atangana would be there soon. She explained about Edoa's baby and what it would take for the tribes to sort that out. Behind his round glasses, Cournarie's eyes lit up; he went off to talk with Bidias in a corner. There was a second step to Damienne's plan—a suicide mission. Before she went, Damienne took a few minutes to gather herself, caressing her amulets. Then she motioned for the Pygmy to follow her.

Her appearance on the veranda was a nonevent. The veranda was raised, like a dais, and should have made her visible to all those natives thirsty for revenge. She descended the stairs, one by one, moving slowly.

Soon she was surrounded by angry natives. That she hadn't been cut to pieces told her something, but Damienne was still nervous, because the trouble with spells are always the exceptions. She wondered what would happen if, for example, one person in the crowd wasn't filled with hatred, didn't see her as an enemy . . . But nothing happened—clearly, all the Bafias felt the same. Still, it pained her to realize that so many people detested her—up until then, she'd only had one known enemy, her brother-in-law, Vivian. As she walked by, she glanced at Abouem's corpse.

🦋

Donenkeng was calm. At the entrance to the village, a group of little girls coming out of the bush with jugs of water balanced on their heads gave Damienne a friendly wave. Clearly, they could see her—too young to share adult hatreds! But Damienne still risked being spotted by other, less naïve people. If even one person raised the alert, she'd be dead. Here, no one could save a white woman. Despite the risks, she kept going and soon came to the shelter where François Bertignac's medical unit had worked. The microscope still stood on the folding table. The syringes that had spread blindness for two years were still lying there on trays, full of tryparsamide. Damienne turned away; the natives already considered the place cursed and they'd avoid it for generations. In front of the chief's compound, she happened across a young blind boy being led by his mother to a stool in the shade beneath a tree where he would eat. The boy wasn't even fifteen. His mother stared in Damienne's direction, but said nothing. Of all the eyes that fell on her during her time in Africa, those hurt Dr. Damienne Bourdin the most, although she wasn't even sure she'd been seen.

Edoa saw her. She was returning from the *marigot* with the midwife when they met by her hut. The women stared at each other, and this time, Damienne didn't avert her eyes, despite all the sympathy she felt for the nurse. When she told her, Edoa fell to the ground. Her cries brought all the mourners from the nearby huts. Without waiting to find out if they saw her or not, Damienne went into Edoa's hut. The medical kit that had saved Bertignac's foot was there in a corner, next to the bed beneath which he'd hidden for eight days. On the bed, swaddled in a pagne, was a beautiful baby. She picked him up. The baby made sucking sounds that reminded Damienne of her own baby, but she quickly brushed the thought aside. She noticed *Raboliot*—a book Damienne hadn't read. She took the book and went back out. Edoa, devastated, was sitting on the ground. Damienne said, "Edoa, it might not be too late. Let's go."

All available pirogues had been requisitioned. They went back and forth across the Sanaga River, ferrying Ewondo warriors. Paramount Chief Atangana was waiting for the last one, accompanied by his retinue of notables and Dr. Jamot.

Jamot was a brave man who'd faced many difficulties and earned the admiration of all; but he was afraid to cross a river in a pirogue. The sight of a river was often enough to make him lose his nerve. And of all the rivers in Cameroon, the Sanaga scared him the most. You couldn't go anywhere without crossing, sometimes more than once, that endless stretch of black water.

Once settled in the boat, Jamot tried to concentrate. He was always careful not to appear frightened in front of natives. Soon, his mind went blank, and he forgot all about the tribal conflict that would explode as soon as they reached the first village on the opposite shore. As the paddle dug into the water, he closed his eyes . . .

Time passed. Suddenly voices rose loudly on the other shore. In the middle of the river, those in the pirogue with Dr. Jamot echoed the cries, but the doctor stayed silent. He was focused inside himself, his eyes closed—he wouldn't open them until he felt the pirogue reach shore. The more his companions shouted and waved, the more the pirogue pitched, the tighter he closed his eyes. This crossing of the

Sanaga seemed longer and more terrifying than usual. Finally, he felt a bump at the front. People jumped into the water on both sides of the pirogue, setting it rocking like a pendulum. Jamot opened his eyes. He thought the war had started.

The Ewondos gathered in a tight group, holding spears aloft and howling, then they rushed at a group of people at the top of a rise. In the middle of the group was a woman with blond hair, a strange belt around her waist, with a Pygmy on one side and a Black woman on the other.

When Jamot saw them, he forgot his fear and jumped out of the pirogue. Damienne Bourdin ran to meet him, leaving Edoa behind, surrounded by her people, wild with joy. Before she reached Jamot, she saw a native in a black tunic with a neat part along his right temple and well-fitted boots on his feet. He nodded politely. Damienne stopped. She was speechless as Paramount Chief Atangana shook her hand and continued toward his niece, whose baby was crying in fright.

As soon as Jamot got out of the Sanaga, he recovered his wits and a good number of his problems as well. Damienne Bourdin had managed to lighten his load, but there was still a heavy weight on his shoulders. She raised her hand in a military salute; Jamot touched his cap and then thought that, all things considered, whoever had sent that darned little bit of a woman, now wearing such a torn, dirty dress, to Africa, hadn't been wrong. She was, like Edoa, like himself, indestructible—at their best when everything goes wrong. The sort of person Jamot was likely to need. Except, for the battle ahead, he knew no one could help him. He'd have to face the administrative machine alone. A machine that, thanks to the medical blunder, had what it needed to settle up once and for all with a medical officer, first class, whose major crime had been to lead, by ministerial decree, a prevention campaign with an enormous budget and, worse, independence. A battle lost before it began.

Damienne sighed with relief. She let her eyes wander downstream, knowing the Sanaga would lead her back to France, since all rivers run to the sea.

IV: The Personal Battle

Clanging pots and pans brought her back to reality.

There, in front of the restaurant that had been built on the site where the Bafia Health Center had stood in colonial days, Damienne Bourdin had relived her first three weeks in Cameroon. Ndongo stood silently by her side—maybe he, too, was lost in his own memories of the same events.

That period had changed her for good, giving Damienne the strength she needed to attain all the honors bestowed upon her since, far beyond the expectations she'd had as a young bourgeois girl, proud and self-centered.

The image of Abouem had never stopped tormenting her. Every night she saw his bloody body in the courtyard of the administrative residence. Abouem—he was really someone. She'd barely met him—no more than a few moments total—and he'd haunted her for thirty years. He'd haunt her to the end of her days. She'd dreamed of possessing him, and blamed herself for his loss. She still wondered if he would have taken such radical action, unleashed his violent revolt, without her intervention that night. Would it have all ended better if she hadn't denounced Pouget?

Only recently had she been able to talk about it with Pierre Charles Cournarie, who'd retired to la Bachellerie, in Périgord. They hadn't answered the question, but Cournarie did thank her for her help bringing peace back to Bafia, which was his jurisdiction. Since then, she'd slept a bit better.

Cournarie told her that Provat, head of what was at the time called "the special agency," had been buried in the courtyard. Damienne had looked all around the subprefecture's courtyard and saw no grave marker. She'd only seen two horses grazing—their excrement, day after day, fertilizing the beautiful lawn that erased all traces of the redhead. He'd been forgotten by everyone—even in Damienne's memories, the only image that remained was of his decapitated body. Were it not for her Pygmy guide, Provat might have ended up in her place, and she in his, six feet underground. She touched her hips and felt, beneath her dress, the amulets of her grigri. She only ever took them off to bathe, to keep them from drying out. The man who'd put them on her long ago, first to protect her out of duty, then to mark her as his property, was beside her now. He stared at her with the same gleeful glow in his eyes as when they'd said goodbye back then, after she'd fulfilled his final obsession. She owed him everything.

"That is called *ndim bako*," he said, pointing at the grigri. "With that, you have nothing to fear from people. But only Jesus Christ will save you," he said in his lilting voice. Because of his accent, Damienne didn't catch all of his words, but his newfound convictions alarmed her. She learned he'd been converted by the Bantus, who were more fervent Christians than most whites. Usually Europeans just lump all the Black peoples in Africa together; it's the natives who classify the different groups. Everyone knows it's a question of honor for a Bantu that they are obviously superior to a Pygmy. Since Damienne had found Ndongo and his clan in an encampment of huts alongside the road, far from their ancestral forest, she suspected she was right to worry that the Bantus were now forcing out the Pygmies, just as they complained the whites had done to them. But when Pygmies are free to wander the virgin forest, their natural habitat, their intellect is second to none. Everything naturally contributes to the fulfilling of their obsessions.

While it was nice to finally speak with Ndongo, Damienne was somewhat disappointed, because the man of her memories, despite speaking only a bizarre dialect, had known how to make himself understood when he spoke of things from his worldview. The Pygmy she'd found now styled himself a French speaker, a Christian, and a citizen; he seemed almost to reproach her for proudly wearing the grigri he'd made, which had consistently proved its worth over the thirty years she'd worn it.

There was nothing left for Damienne to do there in front of the restaurant that insulted history—the history of France's civilizing mission. It was almost time to meet Sikini, she should be on her way. Locals pointed them in the direction of Tamboro, Sikini's neighborhood, and they set off. As they walked, she pulled out the letter that Sikini had her son write, and that the French embassy in Cameroon had forwarded. Beautiful hand-writing: the *b*'s and *g*'s were delicately turned; when two *t*'s were side by side, each was crossed individually; no missing accents. Word of her last book had reached Sikini, so she'd written a letter, just to say hello! It was that little piece of paper that had convinced Damienne to return.

She couldn't say that Sikini had been a friend. Yet because she played a role in Damienne's most cherished memories, she thought of her almost as a long-lost treasure, even though she was still very much alive. Damienne tried to express that when she saw her. Despite her aging, Damienne recognized Sikini immediately. There are things the eye perceives that just can't be faked. The two women fell into each other's arms. Sikini had aged better than Damienne, but there was no hint remaining of her impressive bust. Staring at the woman who'd been one of the most beautiful girls in Bafia, Damienne was more determined than ever to write about aging—the greatest natural disaster in the history of humankind. She gave Sikini the dress she'd promised more than thirty years before, a white-woman's dress, an exquisite evening gown. The former maid would probably never wear it. But that didn't stop her from clutching it to her heart and sobbing—just as she'd sobbed when the two women had last seen each other, in the living room of Cournarie's residence.

Sikini was still sobbing when she introduced her son to Damienne. The young man who'd written the famous letter was well dressed. He was about thirty and was clearly mixed race. His face reminded Damienne of a certain redhead. Damienne put on her brightest smile, cupped her hands around his cheeks and asked his name. Bengoumé à Yakana—he'd been given his maternal grandfather's name, following traditional customary law, since Sikini had never married. As they chatted, Sikini confided that she'd seen Edoa in Yaoundé back in 1946, or maybe 1947. Since then, she'd heard nothing of her. Abouem's son had never returned; he was certainly an Ewondo notable now, if he was still alive.

A long moment of silence passed as Damienne thought about Edoa. Edoa, the indomitable nurse who'd given up everything for love. How many smitten men had trailed behind her, ready to do anything for her: from Abouem and the gendarme Pouget, who wanted to possess her, to Dr. Jamot and Chief Atangana, who wanted to protect her. To find out what became of Edoa, she'd only need to go to her uncle's royal palace, high on the hills of Efoulan in Yaoundé. Damienne was tempted, but quickly decided not to. She'd traveled far and wide and met many extraordinary people, but no one had made as strong an impression on her as Edoa. And so, as far as Edoa was concerned, Damienne preferred to protect her memories.

Damienne stayed at Sikini's home for five days and asked for corn couscous at every meal. Each afternoon, the two women walked through the streets of Bafia; its new Independence Square gave it the feel of a real town, no longer an outpost deep in the forest. The evening before Damienne left, Sikini suggested they go to Donenkeng. They almost did, but Damienne insisted they turn back after she met a blind man sitting in the shade of an avocado tree, who said he'd known Dr. and Madame Monier well.

She'd solved the Vivian problem a long time ago. If he was morose, it wasn't because he was a widower, but because Damienne had made him one of history's losers. He'd chosen her as his enemy in a meaningless battle that she'd let him win—a victory that brought him only money. Her brother-in-law had, as he wished, taken charge of the Bourdin sisters' inheritance, and today he was a rich landowner, living like royalty in his chateau. For decades, he'd had no one left to attack, and Damienne's continued kindness depressed him. Without arguing, without ever showing any disdain, she inflicted a blow from which he would never recover. Instead of fighting him, Damienne opted to fight her own personal battle. Nothing—not jeers or the most traumatic events, not the prestige and respect due to her medical uniform—kept her from becoming a novelist. In truth, what really got Vivian was that he did nothing to contribute to Damienne's success. He would suffer for it for the rest of his days. He would be at the airport waiting for his sister-in-law, and maybe a picture of them would appear in *France-Soir* the following day.

🍂

On the day she leaves, Damienne stands at Dr. Jamot's monument in front of the Ministry of Public Health in the heart of Yaoundé. Ndongo the Pygmy stands by her side for the last time. They both know they'll never see each other again and are overcome with emotion. They haven't spoken all morning, preferring to communicate with gestures alone. The monument to the doctor's glory is immense. The great man, who introduced them in 1929, looks down on them with smiling eyes. Here, on African soil, despite everything, he's given the respect and honor he deserves. Before leaving, Damienne insists on saying one final goodbye to the man who ended his career as a medical officer in the colonial troops: Eugène Jamot, for whom she had the honor of risking her life.

🍂

Today, in Cameroon, in 2020, strangely, it's almost as if the affair of the blind people of Bafia never happened. School textbooks, in which Jamot is described as a hero, don't mention it. So old Bidias was right when he whispered to Cournarie, just before they shot Abouem, "You know, boss, my sister went blind five months ago, and a cousin lost his sight before that. In all our villages, there are people who just woke up and found they'd be blind for the rest of their days. I asked around and no one's seen anything like it among the Bulus or the Makas, though they had as many sick people as we did. What happened is a crime against our tribe, an indefensible crime, and I should be out there in the court-yard getting angry about it with my brothers. But I chose to stay here with you, because you are a good and just boss who listens. I forgive *dokita* Jamot, I know he came here to do good things. Unfortunately, forgiveness isn't as contagious as disease. The anger that reigns here is normal, but it's making us blinder. I hope it will fade, because nothing is eternal. One day, people like Bertignac will be able to come back and eat *kepen* in the village, because everyone loves *kepen*. We're the victims of this story, but not the only ones who deserve pity. Some of us lost our sight; *dokita* Jamot will lose sleep. For the rest of his life, he'll bear the burden of our misfortune because he was determined to help us."

Prophetic words. The scandal of the seven hundred blind people ruined Dr. Eugène Jamot's reputation; he was sent back from Cameroon in 1931 and the mission was ended. He worked for a bit longer in French West Africa, mostly in Ouagadougou, before retiring. And till the day he died, in la Creuse in 1937, the man who fought and over-came sleeping sickness in Africa never forgot what happened in Bafia.

Each year, on April 24, Damienne Bourdin places flowers on his tomb in Sardent.

AUTHOR'S ACKNOWLEDGMENTS

Thank you to Jean-Paul Bado. Reading his important work, *Eugène Jamot 1879–1937, le médecin de la maladie du sommeil ou trypanosomiase*, published in 2011 by Karthala, allowed me to understand how the Jamot Mission worked. Thank you to Pierre Astier. He has supported my project for several years, without giving up, even when doors were shut. Thank you to Emmanuelle Collas. She believed in it.

Mutt-Lon
November 2019

A NOTE FROM THE TRANSLATOR

In this novel, blindness is both fact and metaphor: referencing a horrific and largely forgotten case of medical malpractice from the late 1920s and the ways in which racism limits our ability to see each other and how the past shapes our present. *The Blunder* is not a realist novel, but the history of Eugène Jamot's fight against sleeping sickness in Cameroon frames the novel, which is a send-up of France's "civilizing mission" and a friendly poke at readers, a reminder of the connections between the colonial past and our present day. Mutt-Lon's comedic talent allows him to mine a past tragedy for humor without ever losing sight of the humanity—that amalgam of hubris, altruism, kindness, and blindness—we share with his characters.

The facts: In 1922, Dr. Eugène Jamot was sent to Yaoundé to lead the fight against sleeping sickness, which was decimating villages across Cameroon. At the end of World War I, German Kamerun had been divided into two territories under British and French mandate. Jamot's mission, then, was part of French efforts to establish control over the region. The doctor established a network of mobile units to diagnose and treat the disease. "The blunder" occurred when a junior colleague of Jamot's started injecting patients with higher doses of tryparsamide, an arsenic derivative, which resulted in some seven hundred cases of blindness in the region of Bafia. Despite this, a monument to Dr. Jamot still stands in front of the Ministry of Public Health in Yaoundé.

The metaphors: Blindness points to the folly of colonialism's "mission" and the multiple ways in which pride and ignorance prevent us from seeing the people around us. Without trivializing the real consequences of "the blunder," Mutt-Lon leads us on a picaresque adventure through the forests of colonial-era Cameroon. The plot centers around the misguided exploits of a young French doctor, Damienne Bourdin, who has gone to Cameroon to escape the failures of her own past. Once there, her experiences are shaped as much by her prejudice—what she expects to see—as by the extravagant cast of characters she meets: first and foremost the bungling functionaries who are mainstays of French comedy, but also an array of Cameroonians who both evoke and unsettle stereotypes of the "native." We follow Damienne's footsteps, but she is no hero; while she buys into the idea that she alone can save the day, the plot proves otherwise. Still, as Damienne races through the jungle, shedding her clothes in a send-up of the Tarzan and Jane tropes popularized in the Johnny Weissmuller movies of the 1930s and '40s, we gain insight into the legacy of French colonialism and the blind spots that shape how that history is remembered both in Cameroon and beyond.

In style, *The Blunder* recalls the French tradition of the philosophical tale, popularized in the eighteenth century by Voltaire. Damienne's race against the clock is repeatedly paused as she stops to listen to the stories of each person she meets, from Dr. Jamot to Edoa, the native damsel who is not in distress and who needs no saving. But it is also a novel written in 2020 by a young, French-speaking, Black Cameroonian man—the author's pseudonym, Mutt-Lon, translates as "man of the land"—and he is channeling voices from two eras before his time: the 1960s, when Cameroon was newly independent, and the 1920s, when the French were newly arrived. That means he is writing in a language that both is and isn't his, in voices we need to hear, as he intended, with a wink and ironic distance.

This is particularly important as we confront the outdated and frequently racist language used by some of Mutt-Lon's characters, and his caricatures of colonial clichés, including sexual innuendos that hinge on (and ultimately undercut) racist canards about lascivious natives and desirous white women. Readers may well bridle at some terms used unselfconsciously by the characters, but that *is* the point. He gives voice to characters who reflect the ideology of their time, neither condoning their racism nor silencing them. His characters are not fully fleshed-out individuals, but rather reminders of our own, very present, human imperfections. And Mutt-Lon does this in a way that allows us to share a welcome and necessary laugh.

The translation you now hold is also the product of many conversations, including those I (a not-so-young, English-speaking, white American woman) had with the author about his work, and with others about francophone literature, the history of French colonialism, and our home-grown American racism. Throughout, I sought to faithfully capture Mutt-Lon's style, especially when he seeks to unsettle readers, invoking stereotypes we would relegate to the past but that haunt us still. I apologize for any places where my translation falls short.

When I first read *Les 700 aveugles de Bafia*, at the start of this long Covid lockdown, the novel's boisterous humor felt like a life buoy. I thank Mutt-Lon for entrusting me with his tale and for so kindly responding to my many questions. I am grateful to Raphaël Thierry, of the Astier-Pécher Literary and Film Agency, and to the editors at Amazon Crossing, in particular Liza Darnton, for their support and guidance. Finally, *un grand merci* to the friends and family whose voices make up my day-to-day—especially Jacob, Miriam, and Ben.

Amy B. Reid
September 2021

ABOUT THE AUTHOR

Photo © Thierry Ntamack

Mutt-Lon is the literary pseudonym of author Nsegbe Daniel Alain. His first novel, *Ceux qui sortent dans la nuit* (*Those Who Come Out at Night*, 2013), brought him critical acclaim when it received the prestigious Ahmadou Kourouma Prize in 2014. *Les 700 aveugles de Bafia* (2020), published in English as *The Blunder*, is his third novel and the first to be translated into English. He lives in Douala.

ABOUT THE TRANSLATOR

Photo © 2017 Kim McDonald

Amy B. Reid is an award-winning translator who has worked with authors from Cameroon, Côte d'Ivoire, the Democratic Republic of the Congo, and Haiti. Among her translations are the Patrice Nganang titles *Dog Days: An Animal Chronicle* (2006) and the trilogy comprised of *Mount Pleasant* (2016), *When the Plums Are Ripe* (2019), and *A Trail of Crab Tracks* (2022), as well as *Queen Pokou: Concerto for a Sacrifice* (2009) and *Far from My Father* (2014) by Véronique Tadjo. In 2016 she received a Literature Translation Fellowship from the National Endowment for the Arts for *When the Plums Are Ripe*. She holds a PhD in French from Yale University (1996) and is a professor of French and Gender Studies at New College of Florida.